WASHOE COUNTY LIBRARY

3 1235 03624 8685

Noelle focused her attention on the red velvet bag that Mindy was holding. Then she dipped her hand inside, swirling it around the many slips of paper. The names of every student at North Ridge High — with the exception of those already picked — were in the bag.

Somewhere inside was Charlie's name.

Unless it had already been picked.

Think positive! Noelle scolded herself. *Positive. Positive. Positive. Charlie's name is in this bag. It is! It is! It is! And I will pull it out. I will! I will! I will!* Holding her breath, Noelle closed her eyes and reached into the very bottom of the bag, wrapped her fingers around a slip of paper, and pulled it out.

D1052343

Secret Santa

SABRINA JAMES

Point

Acknowledgments
A Christmas stockingful of thanks to my editor, Abby McAden, who asked me to write _Secret Santa_. Thanks also to my agent, Evan Marshall.

If you purchased this book without a cover, you should be aware that this book is stolen property. It was reported as "unsold and destroyed" to the publisher, and neither the author nor the publisher has received any payment for this "stripped book."

No part of this work may be reproduced, stored in a retrieval system, or transmitted in any form or by any means, electronic, mechanical, photocopying, recording, or otherwise, without written permission of the publisher. For information regarding permission, write to Scholastic Inc., Attention: Permissions Department, 557 Broadway, New York, NY 10012.

ISBN-13: 978-0-439-02695-6
ISBN-10: 0-439-02695-4

Copyright © 2007 by John Scognamiglio

SCHOLASTIC, POINT, and associated logos are trademarks and/or registered trademarks of Scholastic Inc.

Text design by Steve Scott
Text type was set in Plantin

12 11 10 9 8 7 6 5 4 3 2   7 8 9 10 11 12/0

Printed in the U.S.A.
First Scholastic printing, October 2007

Secret Santa

Memo

To: The Students of North Ridge High School
From: Principal Seymour Hicks
Date: Monday, December 19
Subject: Christmas!

This year the entire student body of North Ridge High will be participating in a Secret Santa Exchange. This includes all freshmen, sophomores, juniors, and seniors. There will be no exceptions. Everyone *must* participate.

No inappropriate gifts or contraband is allowed — these will be immediately confiscated. The purpose of the game is to spread the spirit of the season. Spending limits will be outlined in a separate memo distributed during homeroom.

Names will be selected during lunch period and Secret Santas will be revealed this Friday night at the Christmas dance.

Happy Holidays!

Chapter One

"So are you dreaming of a white Christmas?"

Sixteen-year-old Noelle Kramer looked up from the Secret Santa memo she was reading. There had been a stack of them on every table in the cafeteria. She excitedly waved the memo in the air with one hand as her best friend, Lily Norris, slid into the seat next to her with her lunch tray.

Noelle and Lily had been best friends since kindergarten. They had bonded over nail polish, trying to figure out what color their kindergarten teacher, Mrs. Nelson, was wearing on her nails. Noelle had thought it was cherry while Lily had thought it was purple. When they finally worked up the courage to ask Mrs. Nelson the color of her nail polish, she told them it was raspberry, which instantly became Noelle and Lily's favorite color (at least for that year).

After that they were joined at the hip, playing together every day after school, calling each other on the phone, having sleepovers, sharing their toys, and then as they got older, sharing their clothes and innermost secrets. Especially secrets having to do with guys!

"No, I'm not dreaming of a white Christmas," Noelle answered.

"Are visions of sugar plums dancing in your head?"

"No."

"Then explain the dreamy expression I saw on your face." Lily held up a hand. "And please don't tell me it has to do with Charlie."

Noelle bit her lower lip. She *had* been thinking of Charlie. When wasn't she?

She knew the very last thing Lily was going to want to talk about was romance, so she'd have to ease into this.

"Principal Hicks's memo!" she exclaimed.

"I know, I know," Lily groaned. "I saw it. Like I don't have enough people to shop for. Now I have to add another person to my Christmas shopping list. But that still doesn't answer my question."

"Don't you see? This is the chance I've been waiting for."

Lily abandoned the carton of chocolate milk she was getting ready to sip. She gave Noelle a suspicious look — a look Noelle knew *very* well. Noelle didn't even have to say her next words. She knew Lily knew what they were going to be. Often they could read each other's minds.

But Noelle said them anyway.

"I finally have a chance to get Charlie."

Lily groaned and dropped her head on the table, pounding it with a fist. "Charlie? *Charlie?!* Why, why, why, Noelle? Why do you keep doing this to yourself? When are you going to realize that Charlie doesn't even know you exist?"

Ouch! That was a little harsh.

"He does too!" she snapped back.

"Okay, okay, he knows you *exist*," Lily said in an apologetic tone. "He knows you're a living, breathing creature. How could he not? You've been living next door to him since the third grade. But he doesn't see you as anything but the girl next door. Or a little sister. He doesn't see you as girlfriend material!"

"When did you become so grinchy?"

"I'm not trying to hurt your feelings, but you've been crushing on Charlie forever."

It was true. And how could she not? Noelle could still remember the day she first met Charlie. She and Lily had been at the local playground, playing on the monkey bars, when a ten-year-old boy had come over to them and said girls couldn't climb the monkey bars. Noelle said they could and continued to climb until he tried to push her off. Luckily, she hadn't fallen. He tried to push her a second time when all of a sudden a blond-haired boy she had never seen before came to her rescue. He pulled the bully away from her, shoved him to the ground, and told him boys weren't supposed to hit girls and if he ever did it again, *he* would hit *him*! The bully had quickly run from the playground and never bothered Noelle again.

Before Noelle could thank her hero, his mother had called his name and he ran off, giving her a smile and a wave. Noelle would never forget his name: Charlie!

That night her mother told her that a new

family had moved into the house next door and they had two sons. The older son was named Charlie and the younger one was Ryan.

Noelle had gasped. Could *her* Charlie be living next door to her?

She found out the next morning when she and her mother brought a freshly baked blueberry pie over to their new neighbors.

It *was* the same Charlie!

Noelle had wanted to thank Charlie for coming to her rescue the day before. She had wanted to gush. Instead, she had blushed and been tongue-tied the entire time.

And that was still the way she acted around him, eight years later.

Charlie Grant was the most popular senior at North Ridge High School. He was cute, cute, cute, with blond hair, green eyes, and two of the most adorable dimples. He excelled at both sports and academics. He had tons of friends, and he *always* had a different girlfriend. Noelle's theory for his constantly changing girlfriends was that he hadn't found the *right* girl yet.

Her!

"I have a plan!" Noelle announced. "A

foolproof plan that's going to get me exactly what I want for Christmas this year!"

Across the cafeteria, Celia Armstrong watched Noelle Kramer and Lily Norris talk. She knew they were best friends. They ate lunch together every day, and sometimes she saw them shopping at the mall or at the movies. She smothered a sigh and looked away. She wished she had a best friend. Technically, she did, but Crishell was three thousand miles away, living in California, which was where Celia had lived all her life until this past July when her father had gotten a new job and they moved to New York.

It wasn't that Celia didn't have new friends. She did.

But she didn't feel like she knew them.

Or that they knew her.

The *real* her.

She couldn't be *herself* with them. Her guard was always up, and she felt like if she didn't do or say the right thing, it would be a disaster. And she didn't think they liked her even though they acted like they did.

Sometimes the other kids called her Beach

Girl. It wasn't said nastily. It was a nickname given to her because she came from California and well, she looked like a beach girl. She was tall and willowy, with shoulder-length sun-streaked hair and sky-blue eyes. Coming from California, she had lived on the beach most of her life. She loved surfboarding, parasailing, swimming, scuba diving, and volleyball.

But you couldn't do any of that stuff when you lived on the East Coast. Once the summer was over, that was it. Back home, you could do those things all year round.

This time last year she was a freshman at Malibu High with friends she had had since kindergarten. Now she was a sophomore at North Ridge High and feeling like an outsider.

She knew she shouldn't be complaining.

She was one of the most popular girls at North Ridge High. There was just one problem.

She didn't want to be popular!

It wasn't like she had *planned* to become popular. It just happened!

Celia and her parents had moved to North Ridge, a small suburb of New York City, that July. Their new house was in North Ridge Heights, a gated community where most of her

7

parents' new coworkers lived. Upon their arrival, a welcome-to-the-neighborhood party had been thrown.

It was at this party that Celia met the only two girls there who were her age: Amber Davenport and Shawna Westin.

If there was one word to describe Amber, it was gorgeous. She had a mane of wavy jet-black hair, smoky-brown eyes, and always dressed like she had stepped out of the pages of a fashion magazine. Shawna, also a brunette but with a short bob and bangs, was dressed just as impeccably as Amber. Both were wearing cropped tops, short skirts, and shoes that looked like the ones Heidi wore on *The Hills*. Could they really afford shoes that expensive? (The answer, Celia soon found out, was yes, thanks to one magic phrase: *parents' credit card.*)

Celia, in her cutoff shorts, flip-flops, and T-shirt, her hair pulled back in a messy ponytail, felt like a bit of a slob.

But for whatever reason, Amber and Shawna talked with her, and when the party was over, Amber had invited Celia to come over to her house the following afternoon. With nothing else to do, Celia had accepted the invitation.

And that's when it all started.

Her road to popularity.

After spending the afternoon at Amber's — looking back — Celia now realized it had been some sort of test. Amber and Shawna had kept asking her questions — *What's your favorite TV show? Who's your favorite band? What designers do you like to wear? What do you do for fun?* — and she had kept answering. Apparently she had passed the test because within days she was being invited by Amber and Shawna to go to the beach, the country club, the movies, shopping in Manhattan. With no friends, Celia kept accepting their invitations and before she knew it became part of their group. They gave one another their own ring tones on their cell phones, IM-ed when they were online, text-messaged, and went shopping for new wardrobes before classes started.

It was during this shopping trip that Celia started to wonder if maybe she had made a mistake . . .

When Celia dressed, she dressed for comfort. She liked wearing loose tops, T-shirts, jeans. She absolutely *hated* high heels of any sort — because she was so tall — and didn't wear them unless she had to. She didn't need the extra height.

Every time she pulled something she liked off a shelf or rack, Amber would shake her head sadly and give a disapproving sigh. Then Amber would take Celia's choice, put it back, and select something else, urging Celia to try it on.

Which Celia did.

Then when she would come out wearing it, Amber and Shawna would both ooh and aah, telling her how great she looked.

And so she would buy it.

Again and again and again, until she had a brand-new wardrobe that she never would have bought on her own.

When she got home that night and looked at all her purchases, she could barely remember trying all the different outfits on, let alone buying them.

It was like she was powerless!

Hypnotized into doing Amber's bidding!

She could return everything and buy the things she originally wanted, but then what would happen when Amber and Shawna asked why she wasn't wearing her new clothes?

She didn't want to get on Amber's bad side. She already knew she had a temper. Not only from the way she spoke to the clerks in the stores they had shopped in, but the way she sometimes spoke to Shawna. Like she was an idiot. And Shawna took it. She never talked back. Celia had discussed it all with Crishell the last time they were on the phone.

"Sounds like Amber's a queen bee, and you don't want to mess with one of those," Crishell said. "They sting! Obviously Shawna does whatever Amber wants. She probably doesn't have a choice, she's been so beaten down, but you do. Once classes start you'll make some other friends and you can say bye-bye to Amber."

But Celia hadn't been able to say good-bye.

It wasn't until she started her sophomore year in September that she learned Amber and Shawna were two of the most popular girls at North Ridge High. When they walked down the hallways, the crowds instantly parted. Everyone knew their names. Girls were constantly coming up to them, trying to become their friend, inviting them to parties, complimenting them on their hair, their makeup, their clothes. Guys did the same things, often asking them if they needed a ride or if they wanted to go out sometime.

And because she was always with Amber and Shawna, she was considered to be just as important as they were.

Amber and Shawna had chosen *her* to be their friend.

And because of that, *their* friends were now *her* friends.

She was accepted without question. She didn't have to "prove" herself to anyone.

As a result, she was constantly being invited to parties, too. She could never say no because Amber would immediately start making a plan for them: what they would wear, how they would do their hair, how long they would stay, where they would go afterward.

And so Celia's life became nothing but non-stop parties on the weekends and hanging out with pretty girls and good-looking guys during the week.

It meant sitting at the same table at lunch every day with Amber and Shawna.

It meant hanging out with them after school.

And it meant she couldn't be friends with the people she wanted to be friends with because they weren't part of the cliques that Amber and Shawna hung out with. Celia didn't even have to ask. She just *knew*. If she told Amber she wanted to eat lunch with Hannah Langston, who was in her English Lit class and loved Jane Austen as much as she did, Amber would look at her like she had three heads. Because in Amber's mind, Hannah wasn't considered pretty and popular, so why would she want to spend time with her? Hannah always had her nose buried in a book. Boring! The same with Freddy Keenan, her lab partner. He was considered a nerd because he got good grades and didn't play sports.

How had her life become so complicated?

It wasn't that she didn't like Amber and Shawna. They were nice. Sometimes. But she didn't feel like she had a lot in common with them. Her life didn't revolve around the latest fashion magazines. It didn't revolve around parties or trying to get the attention of guys. And she didn't like making fun of people the way Amber did. Amber didn't do it in an obvious way, but she was always criticizing. Always making jokes. Always trying to put someone down.

And somehow, that person always knew.

Amber even did it to Shawna.

That wasn't who Celia was.

But she didn't know what to do.

If she broke away from Amber and Shawna, Amber could turn her wrath on her. And then where would she be?

She'd have *no* friends.

And forget about having a boyfriend.

Not that she was looking for one.

And not that she wanted one, although Amber and Shawna thought she should have one and were constantly trying to fix her up.

Amber and Shawna both had boyfriends — track star Simon Larson was Amber's boyfriend, while Shawna was dating Connor Hughes, who was on the basketball team.

It was nice of Amber and Shawna to keep setting her up on dates, but the guys they kept setting her up with weren't her type. She didn't have a thing for jocks or for preppy, good-looking guys who were constantly checking themselves out in mirrors, making sure their hair was all in place and their shirts weren't wrinkled. She wanted to go out with a guy who had something to say. A guy who had thoughts and ideas and liked talking and debating and arguing. A guy who had lots of different interests and who wasn't afraid of being himself.

There *was* a guy at North Ridge High who was all that.

And Celia had a crush on him. A small one. Not a big one. She'd only started thinking of him romantically in the last month, after suffering through all the blind dates she'd been on.

But it would be social suicide if she decided to date him. Amber and Shawna would *flip* out.

But would that be so bad?

Especially if it meant going out with a guy *she* was interested in.

Celia needed to think this over. Although a part of her was tempted to just be herself and break free of Amber and Shawna, another part of her wasn't ready to do it. Not yet.

But soon.

Very soon.

Chapter Two

"Who do you think is hotter?" David Benson asked. "Batgirl or Wonder Woman?"

Froggy Keenan thought about the question carefully before answering. He took a spoonful of his chocolate pudding and carefully slipped it into his mouth, savoring the flavor. "Are you talking about Batgirl from the comics or Alicia Silverstone in *Batman & Robin*?"

"Alicia Silverstone was a babe in *Clueless*, but she was totally miscast as Batgirl in *Batman & Robin*. She didn't have the bod for it."

"What about the Batgirl from the TV series from the sixties?"

"Hot, but not as hot as Julie Newmar's Catwoman. *Meow!*"

"True, but no Catwoman was as hot as Michelle Pfeiffer," Froggy countered.

"Definitely," David agreed. "She made Halle Berry's Catwoman look like kitty litter! But getting back to the original question. Who's hotter? Batgirl from the comics or Wonder Woman from the comics?"

"Wonder Woman," Froggy instantly answered. "No question."

"I agree! So when is Hollywood going to make the movie version? They've already done Superman and Batman a bunch of times. We need to see a hot super-chick on the big screen!"

"Wonder Woman does have nice assets," Froggy said. "Did you know the TV series from the seventies is out on DVD?"

"My dad owns all of them. He told me he used to watch it every Friday night when he was kid."

"Mine too! He also used to watch *The Incredible Hulk*. He says the TV show was way better than the movie."

"The movie was a snoozefest, but it wasn't as bad as *The Fantastic Four*."

"Or *Daredevil*."

"Or *Elektra*."

It went without saying that Froggy and his best friend were comic-book geeks. Or that the Sci-Fi Channel was their favorite. They were also fans of *Star Trek*, *Battlestar Galactica* (the original series and the new version), *Hercules*, *Xena: Warrior Princess* (Lucy Lawless was *hot*!), and *Star Wars* (the movies that were made in the late seventies and early eighties. Not the prequels that were made in the nineties). But because of all this, when it came to the North Ridge High food chain, Froggy and David were at the bottom. Way at the bottom.

They were nerds.

Of course, Froggy didn't consider himself and David to be nerds even though they had a lot of characteristics that were considered . . . nerdy. Among those characteristics: They were very smart and members of the National Honor Society. They were already taking advance placement classes (David was taking A.P. Biology and Froggy was taking A.P. History). They weren't jocks. And they weren't the best dressers.

Girls at North Ridge treated them as though they were invisible.

But that didn't stop David.

When Froggy thought of his best friend, one word constantly came to mind. Determined. When David wanted something, he went after it. When they were in fifth grade and William Shatner was going to be at a local bookstore signing his autobiography, David made sure he was the first person in line. When tickets went on sale for *Spider-Man 3*, David got a ticket to the opening show, as well as one for Froggy.

So when it came to girls and dating, David never had any problems going up to a girl he liked and asking her out.

The only problem was, they never said yes.

Compared to the other guys at North Ridge High, David was short. He was also thin. And his clothes were very baggy. He didn't have the look of an Abercrombie & Fitch model like most of the jocks at North Ridge High. His hair, which was an orangey carrot color, was short and spiky. He looked more like Anthony Michael Hall's character in *Sixteen Candles*. The nerd.

Froggy knew he wasn't a hunk either, but he didn't think he looked nerdy. He was an average-looking guy. He wore his light brown hair in a buzz cut and he pretty much wore plaid shirts, jeans, and sneakers.

Of course, there was his nickname.

A nickname that made you think of something slimy.

Even though Froggy's real name was Frederick, his classmates called him Froggy. They'd been doing it for such a long time that most couldn't remember how the nickname had started. Some thought it was because of the glasses he wore, which magnified his brown eyes; others thought maybe it was because he liked the color green. There *was* a reason, but Froggy wasn't about to remind anyone of it.

Being on the outside looking in didn't really bother him.

Well, it hadn't until recently.

David waved Principal Hicks's memo in his face, startling him from his thoughts. "Did you take a look at this? It's a golden opportunity!"

"Huh?"

"The Christmas dance!"

"What about it?"

"What's the first thing that pops into your head when you think about Christmas?"

"Santa Claus?"

"No!"

"Presents?"

"No!"

"Candy canes?"

"NO!"

"Then what? What?" Froggy asked, exasperated. "Give me a little help here. The bell for next class is about to ring. I could be guessing all day."

"Mistletoe!" David exclaimed.

The lightbulb went on over Froggy's head as he realized the direction David's thoughts had headed. "Ah . . . mistletoe."

David slammed Froggy on the back. "Yes, mistletoe! I bet there's going to be lots of it hanging up at the dance. Which means lots of opportunity for kissing!" David rubbed his hands together and gave an evil Bart Simpson chuckle. "No female lips will be safe from me on Friday night!" He started making loud kissing sounds.

"Better be careful of who you kiss," Froggy warned. "Especially if she has a boyfriend!"

"If you could go out with any girl in our sophomore class, who would it be?" David asked.

Froggy shrugged. "I don't know."

"Come on! Give me some names. You can't tell me you haven't noticed how hot some of the girls have gotten since freshman year."

"Amber and Shawna are pretty hot," Froggy said.

"Reality check! They don't even know we exist. Give me another name."

Froggy gazed around the cafeteria. Then his eyes stopped. "Celia's a babe."

David followed Froggy's gaze and nodded his head approvingly. "Totally. Beach Girl is definitely a babe. And she's not dating anyone."

Froggy did a double take. "She isn't? I was at the movies last week and I thought I saw her with a guy. He had his arm around her shoulders and kept pulling her close."

David rolled his eyes. "Amber and Shawna keep setting her up on dates with lunkheads from the Jock Squad. When are they going to realize that brains matter more than brawn?" David playfully punched Froggy on his shoulder. "Maybe you should ask Celia out."

Froggy blushed and quickly slipped another spoonful of chocolate pudding into his mouth so he wouldn't have to answer.

"Have you noticed that Celia Armstrong keeps staring at us?" Noelle whispered to Lily. Noelle didn't know why she had whispered. Celia was sitting all the way across the cafeteria. Maybe it was because she was one of the "popular" girls, and the popular girls ruled North Ridge High.

Lily shrugged, tossing her long red curls over one shoulder. "Maybe we're both walking fashion disasters and Beach Girl is in shock."

"Don't be so mean! She has a name. And she seems kind of nice. Not as stuck-up as Amber and Shawna."

"Don't be fooled," Lily warned, her green eyes narrowing. "If she's friends with them she's just as evil as they are." Lily took a sip of her chocolate milk. "So what's your plan? Don't keep me in suspense. I'm dying to know."

"Are you serious or are you just being sarcastic?"

Lily crossed her heart. "Totally serious. I swear."

"It has to do with Principal Hicks's memo."

"What about it?"

"I know you disagree, but I think it's kind of nice. It spreads Christmas cheer. And it's a great opportunity for Christmas romance."

Lily held up two fingers and hissed liked a vampire. "Don't mention the word romance to me. Not after what Jason did to me this summer!"

"Oops! Sorry!"

Noelle knew that Lily's breakup with her boyfriend, Jason Fitzpatrick, was still a sore point. That summer Jason had been working as a camp counselor at a sleepaway camp in Massachusetts. Even though he'd been calling and emailing Lily when he first went away, he eventually stopped. Lily didn't think anything of it. She just assumed it was because he was busy, but it wasn't. Oh, he was busy alright — *getting* busy with another girl!

Of course, Lily had absolutely no idea that Jason was romancing another girl until he returned home and promptly broke up with her via email. Email! He couldn't even do it in person! And poor Lily had been waiting to go over to his place with a plate of homemade oatmeal cookies (Jason's favorites) wearing a new outfit she had bought that day just for his homecoming. For weeks she had had the day of his homecoming circled with a pink heart on her calendar.

Noelle could still remember the pain and hurt on Lily's face. It had been a Saturday night and she had been watching a *Project Runway* marathon on Bravo. Her parents had gone out for dinner and she'd been home alone, nestled on the couch, the air conditioner running, munching some freshly popped popcorn. The ringing doorbell had taken her totally by surprise because she hadn't been expecting anyone. When she opened the front door and saw Lily standing there, looking like she was in shock, she instantly knew something was wrong.

"What happened?" she asked, rushing to Lily's side and pulling her into a hug.

That was all it had taken for Lily to burst into tears and tell her everything.

Noelle had been outraged for her best friend. How could Jason do such a thing?

After Lily had cried her heart out — using up an entire box of Kleenex in the process — Noelle had ordered in a pizza with extra mushrooms (Lily's favorite) and then told Lily she was staying overnight.

They stayed up until three A.M. — Lily ranting and raving about Jason, and Noelle just listening. Over the next few weeks Noelle made sure she and Lily did lots of fun things together. Manicures. Pedicures. Shopping for shoes. Renting a bunch of DVDs. Having sleepovers.

Little by little Lily started returning to her old self, although Noelle knew it was still going to be a while before Lily trusted a guy again. Jason had been the first guy she had dated exclusively. They'd been going out for five months since the Valentine's Day dance — their first date — before he left for the summer. Even though Noelle hadn't had a date for the Valentine's Day dance and had stayed home — secretly wishing that Charlie was going to ask her at the last minute. Of course, he didn't — she'd been thrilled for Lily and told her to call her the second Jason brought her home so she could tell her *everything*. (Lily called her at 12:01 A.M., a minute after her curfew, and kept Noelle on the phone for an hour, telling her every romantic thing Jason had done until their fathers made them hang up because they were both talking so loudly.)

Noelle knew Lily had been totally blindsided when Jason dumped her and felt like an idiot for not figuring out there was another girl. To make matters worse, Jason's new girlfriend was a girl who also went to their high school. It wasn't even a girl from another high school or even another state! It was Sonia Lopez, who looked like she could be Eva Longoria's younger sister. So not only did Lily have a broken heart, she got to see Jason and Sonia together every day at school.

Noelle was a romantic at heart. Things hadn't worked out between Lily and Jason, but that was because their relationship hadn't been meant to be.

It also meant the right guy was still out there, waiting for Lily.

She was determined to restore Lily's faith in love so she would one day find that guy.

And she knew just how to do it.

By finally getting Charlie for herself.

Noelle pointed out Mindy Yee, who was going from table to table with a red velvet bag. Inside the bag were the names of the entire student body of North Ridge High. "That's my plan."

"Huh?"

"I'm going to pick Charlie's name. I'm going to be his Secret Santa."

Lily gave Noelle an incredulous look. "Do you know how many names are in that bag? Your chances of pulling out Charlie's name are slim to none!"

"Oh, really?" Noelle said with determination. "Just watch me!"

Chapter Three

"It's Secret Santa time!" Mindy Yee announced, shaking the red velvet bag she was holding. "Who wants to go first?"

"I will," Lily grumbled. "Might as well get this over with." She dipped her hand into the open bag, pulled out a name, and promptly stuck it in her pocket.

"Aren't you going to look to see who you got?" Noelle asked, dying of curiosity.

"I'll do it later," Lily said. "Right now I want to see you pull out the name you're so sure you're going to get."

"And who might that be?" Mindy asked.

Noelle stuck her tongue out at Lily. "No one special," she said, knowing that Mindy was the biggest gossip at North Ridge High and if she said she was hoping to pull out Charlie's name, the entire school would know by the end of the day. And wouldn't that be special? Not! She wanted to be the one who told Charlie she had feelings for him, and she wanted everything to be perfect when that day finally arrived.

And it was all going to start with her being his Secret Santa.

Noelle focused her attention on the red velvet bag that Mindy was holding. Then she dipped her hand inside, swirling it around the many slips of paper. The names of every student at North Ridge High — with the exception of those already picked — were in the bag.

Somewhere inside was Charlie's name.

Unless it had already been picked.

Think positive! Noelle scolded herself. *Positive. Positive. Positive. Charlie's name is in this bag. It is! It is! It is! And I will pull it out. I will! I will! I will!*

Holding her breath, Noelle closed her eyes and reached into the very bottom of the bag, wrapped her fingers around a slip of paper, and pulled it out. Once she was done, Mindy moved down the table to the others who were waiting.

"So, who did you get?" Lily asked.

Noelle was almost afraid to look at the slip. It had to be Charlie. If it wasn't, she was going to be so disappointed.

"Charlie, Charlie, Charlie," she chanted under her breath as she opened her eyes and unfolded the slip of paper she had chosen.

Noelle's shoulders slumped and she gave a sigh of disappointment when she saw the typed name.

It wasn't Charlie.

"Don't keep me in suspense!" Lily urged. "Tell me who you picked!"

"You jinxed me!" Noelle wailed, waving the slip of paper in front of Lily's face. Lily promptly snatched it out of her hands and read it.

"Well, you came close," she said, handing it back. "You did get a Grant."

"But not the Grant I wanted!"

Noelle had picked the name of Charlie's younger brother, Ryan, who was also a sophomore.

"I don't want to say I told you so, but I told you so," Lily singsonged.

Noelle's temper flared. "You don't have to rub it in!"

"Hey, I was only teasing!" Lily apologized.

"Come on, Noelle! Did you really think you were going to pull out his name?"

"Yes, I did!"

When it came to love and romance, Noelle felt that you had to believe. Otherwise what was the point? All the heroines in the romantic comedies she loved to rent, like Elle Woods in *Legally Blonde*, made what they wanted happen!

She was no different. So she hadn't picked Charlie's name. She was still going to let him know how she felt about him.

And she was going to tell him the night of the Christmas dance.

Celia couldn't believe it.

She was *so* excited.

She stared at the slip of paper in her hands to make sure she wasn't imagining it. That her eyes weren't playing tricks on her.

But the name was still the same.

Jake Morrisey.

The guy she was crushing on!

She really hadn't had any sort of expectations when she'd reached into the bag Mindy was holding out. She'd gotten a copy of Principal Hicks's memo like everyone else and figured she'd pull a name, buy a gift, and that would be that.

It never even occurred to her that she could pull out Jake's name.

But she had!

Now she had a chance to let Jake know how she felt about him.

She couldn't wait to tell Crishell tonight. She wished she had someone to tell right now, but other than Amber and Shawna, she really didn't have any close friends. If she were friends with Noelle and Lily, maybe she would tell them, but they weren't. She had noticed Noelle and Lily picking their names earlier. Noelle hadn't looked too happy with who she'd gotten, and Lily hadn't even bothered looking at the name she'd pulled. What was up with that?

Every so often she would smile at Noelle and Lily in the hopes of getting a smile back, but she never did. It was almost like they were afraid of her. And she knew the reason why.

Amber and Shawna.

Celia sighed as she thought of them. She knew they were going to want to know who she had picked and she wasn't sure what she was going to do. Knowing Amber, she probably had some strategy already mapped out when it came to their Secret Santas and she and Shawna would have to follow it.

Sometimes Celia wondered if Shawna felt the same way she did about Amber. If she resented her bossiness. She thought she might. It was just a feeling she had. But she didn't dare ask Shawna. What if she was wrong?

Just then, almost as if she had wished for their presence, Amber and Shawna came walking out of the cafeteria, designer tote bags filled with the books for their afternoon classes tossed over one shoulder, oversized sunglasses perched on their noses (even though they were inside and it was a cloudy day), looking like two celebutantes. Amber was wearing a low-cut, leopard-chiffon top with puff sleeves, a black pencil-skirt, and black slouch boots, while Shawna was in a V-neck, long-sleeve black top with a white bubble skirt. As usual, Celia felt underdressed when standing next to them, even though she had liked her outfit when she'd chosen it that morning. Today she was wearing a violet turtleneck, gray plaid pleated skirt, and purple suede peep-toe shoes.

They hadn't had lunch together today because there had been an emergency meeting of the cheerleading squad and all the cheerleaders, including Amber and Shawna, had eaten together. Amber and Shawna had tried to get Celia to try out for the squad in September, but she had passed, telling them she didn't think she'd be as good as they were.

Amber peered at Celia over the rims of her sunglasses. "Are those split ends, I see, Celia? We're going to have to make an appointment for you with Javi. She'll fix you right up. Friday night is the dance and we're going to have to look our best. I figured we could all get our hair done Friday afternoon. Manis and pedis, too. In Manhattan. My treat. Daddy will have a limo take us. No Metro North for us! Those trains will be crazy with last-minute holiday shoppers."

"Oooh!" Shawna squealed, clapping her hands excitedly. "Fun!"

Amber whipped out her cell phone. "I'm going to call now and make our appointments. Is there anything else you want done, Celia? A facial? Massage?"

Celia shook her head, suddenly feeling guilty

for the not-so-nice thoughts she'd been having about Amber. Why did she always forget about the *nice* side of Amber? Just when Celia thought she couldn't stand her anymore, she did something like this. She was always so generous, constantly inviting Shawna and Celia to rock concerts, movie premieres, the theater, and weekend getaways to her family's second house in Pennsylvania, where there was skiing. When she was cleaning out her closets, she always gave Shawna and Celia first dibs on the clothes, shoes, and accessories she was getting rid of.

Of course, it helped that her father worked on Wall Street and made oodles of money. And Amber was an only child who was spoiled rotten.

Still, she didn't have to share with her friends.

But she did.

That had to mean there was some good in her, right?

Shawna took off her sunglasses and tossed them in her bag. "So, who'd you guys get to be a Secret Santa for?"

Celia was about to answer Shawna's question

when Amber clicked shut her cell phone and announced, "Celia got Charlie Grant!"

Across the hall Noelle couldn't believe her ears.

She couldn't have heard correctly.

Could she?

Celia Armstrong was Charlie's Secret Santa?

Amber's words echoed in her mind.

Celia got Charlie Grant. Celia got Charlie Grant.

CELIA GOT CHARLIE GRANT.

No.

No.

No!!!

How could this have happened?

How could fate be so cruel?!

She stopped in her tracks and Lily bumped into her. "Hey, what's with the lack of motion?"

Noelle turned around and pulled Lily by the arm to one side of the hallway.

"You'll never guess what I just heard," she whispered, making sure the coast was clear. She didn't want anyone else hearing this, especially Mindy Yee, who was known for eavesdropping.

Lily's green eyes lit up. If there was one

thing she loved, it was gossip. "What? What? Spill, spill!"

"I know who Charlie's Secret Santa is."

"Who?"

"Celia Armstrong!"

Lily sighed. "Wouldn't you know it? It makes perfect sense. She's pretty. She's popular. She's just Charlie's type."

Noelle hated to admit it, but Lily was right. Celia was *exactly* Charlie's type. His girlfriends were always gorgeous. They were always popular. He never went out with a girl who was *ordinary*.

Like her.

With her shoulder-length hair and matching chocolate-brown eyes, she was ordinary with a capital O. She knew she was pretty, but she didn't have that extra sparkle, that extra *zing!* that certain girls had that made guys flock around them like bees around honey.

Charlie always went out with girls like that.

But that didn't mean she didn't have a chance.

There was always a first time.

"I bet he's going to fall in love with her the night of the Christmas dance," Lily said.

"Thanks *so* much for trying to cheer me up," Noelle stated. "You are my best friend, right?"

"Hey, I'm just telling you the facts as I see them."

"Facts can sometimes be changed," Noelle said, a determined look on her face.

"Changed? How?"

"I've known Charlie for eight years. Who knows him better than me?"

Lily thought about it for a second. "Outside his family? Probably no one."

"Precisely! So even though I'm not Charlie's Secret Santa, there's nothing stopping me from leaving him gifts."

Lily gave Noelle a confused look. "Huh? But if you leave him gifts isn't he going to think they're from Celia?"

"My gifts are all going to have some sort of personal connection to Charlie," Noelle explained, revealing the plan she'd come up with. "The night of the dance, I'll be able to prove that I'm the one who sent them to him. Celia's not going to be able to do that. My gifts will have *meaning*. And I'll tell Charlie that I was too shy to tell him how I really felt and so I used the Secret Santa game as a way of letting him know my true feelings! How will he be able to resist that? It's like something straight out of a movie!"

"I think you've been watching too many movies," Lily stated dryly. "Okay, I'm going to say something and I don't want you to get mad at me. Promise?"

"When have I ever gotten mad at you?"

"How far back would you like me to go?" Lily started counting off on her fingers. "There was the time in fourth grade when I didn't pick you to be my partner for the class trip because I had a crush on Zach Goodson and I wanted him to be my partner. The time in seventh grade when I wouldn't lend you my sister Vanessa's high heels because I knew you couldn't walk in them and would probably break them. Which you did when I finally did lend them to you so you'd stop being mad at me! The time in eighth grade when I told you I didn't like your graduation dress because I thought the color was all wrong. Then there was the time you got a perm, dyed your hair red, and made the mistake of giving yourself a spray-on tan that made your skin the color of a pumpkin." Lily crossed her arms over her chest. "Would you like me to go on?"

"Okay, okay, so we've had a few spats over the years. We're still friends, aren't we?"

"Best friends," Lily stated. "And I'm only saying this *because* I'm your best friend and because I care about you. It has nothing to do with Jason and my broken heart and my down-with-romance feelings." Lily was quiet for a second. Then she asked, "What happens if after you do all this, Charlie still doesn't like you?"

"What?"

"You like Charlie. You've been obsessed with him for years —"

Noelle cut Lily off. "I'm not obsessed with him! If I was obsessed with him, I'd be stalking him all the time, my bedroom walls would be plastered with pictures of him, and my notebooks would be filled with hearts that say N.K. loves C.G. I'd be boiling bunnies on his stove!"

"I understand the whole knight in shining armor thing," Lily said. "I was at the playground that day when he came to your rescue. But what else is there? Other than his good looks."

"How do I explain it? Yes, he's hot, but you don't get to hang around Charlie as much as I do since we live right next door to each other. I get to see him all the time with his family. Sometimes he's goofy and silly. Other times he's kind and thoughtful. When I'm able to hang out with him, like if our families are having a barbecue together or there's a party, he makes me laugh." Noelle shrugged. "I just like him, and when I think about being with someone, of having a boyfriend, I think of him."

"But is he going think of you as more than just a friend after all these years?" Lily asked.

"That's the problem!" Noelle exclaimed. "Because we're neighbors, he probably doesn't think of me as anything *but* the girl next door. He probably doesn't know that I have feelings for him. And if he's ever had feelings for me, he's probably brushed them to one side."

"That's a pretty big if," Lily said.

"What do I have to lose? At least I have a plan. I'm finally going to do something about my feelings for Charlie. One way or another I'll know by Friday night whether or not I have a future with him. And if I don't, well, I'll be joining you in the down-with-romance club."

Lily gave Noelle a hug. "I don't mean to be a wet blanket. I just don't want you to get hurt. I've been there. I know what it feels like. And I suppose your plan could work," she reluctantly admitted.

"Yes!" Noelle gushed. "It *will* work. And when you see that it does, you'll be ready to give romance another try."

"I doubt it," Lily grumbled as her ex-boyfriend, Jason, walked by with his arm wrapped around the waist of Sonia Lopez.

"What did you say?" Celia asked Amber, not sure she'd heard her correctly. She couldn't have said what she did, could she?

It made no sense.

She *wasn't* Charlie Grant's Secret Santa.

She was Jake's.

"I'm not Charlie Grant's Secret Santa," she said as she walked with Amber and Shawna down the hallway to her next class. "Why did you say that?"

Amber stopped walking, causing Shawna and Celia to also stop. Amber looked around the hallway to make sure they couldn't be overheard. Then she leaned in close to Celia and whispered in her ear, "You *are* Charlie Grant's Secret Santa."

"But I didn't pick his name!"

"Yes, you did," Amber explained, placing a slip of paper into Celia's hand.

Celia knew whose name was going to be on it. She didn't even have to look at it.

But she did.

And she was right.

Charlie Grant.

"I asked Mindy Yee to pull the names of the three hottest seniors out of the bag ahead of time," Amber explained. "They're great boyfriend material. And we can't be Secret Santas to just anyone!"

"B-b-but that defeats the whole purpose of being a Secret Santa!" Celia sputtered. "Besides, you and Shawna already have boyfriends."

"Who are sophomores," Amber sniffed disdainfully.

That hadn't seemed to bother Amber in October at her Halloween party when Simon had asked her out on a date, Celia recalled. It was the first time she'd ever seen Amber genuinely excited. But maybe now she wanted to move up to a senior. And after that? A college freshman?

"You can give me the name you already picked and I'll have Mindy slip it back into the bag."

Celia's stomach dropped.

Give up Jake?

Absolutely positively not!

This was one time when she was going to stand up to Amber no matter what the consequences!

Of course, there was a certain way to handling Amber. You couldn't ever let her think you were defying her or going against her wishes. Uh-uh. No way. She always had to believe that she was in charge and calling the shots.

Or else.

Celia knew she had to be careful with her next words. The last thing she wanted to do was piss off Amber. She noticed that Shawna had been quiet during the entire conversation, which made Celia wonder if Shawna really wanted to be a senior's Secret Santa. After all, she'd been dating Connor since the summer. They seemed like they were happy together, but maybe they weren't.

"I know you guys are looking out for me," Celia said, looking directly into Amber's face. She couldn't look down or away because that would make it look like she was scared of Amber — even though she was! Her heart was pounding like crazy — because then Amber would pounce like a cat chasing a mouse and she'd be dead. She tried to keep her voice calm and steady. "But I'm really into Christmas and having someone else pick my Secret Santa spoils it for me. As cool as Charlie is, I can't be his Secret Santa."

"Whose name did you get?" Amber casually asked. "It must be someone pretty special if you don't want to give them up for Charlie. I'm guessing it's a guy? Maybe a guy who you like? It is, isn't it? Have you been holding out on us, Celia? Keeping secrets? Who is it? You can tell us."

Celia gulped, stunned at how Amber was able to figure things out when she hadn't even given her a single clue!

Celia knew she couldn't weaken. If she did, it was all over and any chance she had with Jake would be gone.

"You know I can't tell you!" she laughed. "It's all part of the Secret Santa game. It would spoil the surprise. You'll find out at the dance!"

And with those words, Celia handed the slip of paper with Charlie's name on it to Shawna. She was afraid if she tried to hand it back to Amber, her hand would shake and she'd be a goner. Amber was staring at her so intently, she felt like she was being studied under a microscope.

"I guess we'll just have to wait until Friday night," Amber said. "Who knew you were so into holiday games?"

Luckily, the bell for next period rang and Celia raced down the hall to her next class, Anatomy and Physiology. Even though she'd been dreading today's class because they were going to be dissecting a pig, anything was better than being dissected by Amber!

"Well, I guess Charlie's name goes back into the Secret Santa bag," Shawna said after Celia left. She was waiting for Amber to have a meltdown. It wasn't very often that someone didn't do what she wanted, and Celia had told her she wasn't going to do what she wanted. It had been such fun to watch! Even though Amber had kept her cool, Shawna could see that she was pissed off. It was the little things that she knew to look for. The slight narrowing of Amber's eyes. The digging of her nails into the palms of her hands. The tap, tap, tapping of her boot on the floor.

Shawna hated to admit it, but she really admired the way Celia had stood up to Amber. She wished she had the courage to do the same thing, but she didn't. No matter what Amber wanted, they did. No questions asked.

There had been a time when their friendship was more of a partnership. Where they took turns making decisions. But in the last year, it was always what Amber wanted.

And Shawna was starting to resent it.

But what else was she going to do?

She couldn't *not* be friends with Amber. That would be social suicide. They were inseparable. They'd been the two most popular girls in grammar school, junior high, and now high school. When people said their names, they didn't say Amber and Shawna. They said *AmberandShawna*. They had a whole social network of friends. And it wasn't that she didn't want to still be friends with Amber. She was just tired of having her call all the shots.

Like with the Secret Santas.

She could care less about going out with a senior, but Amber recently made the decision that they needed to go out with older guys. She hadn't made the decision without a reason.

Amber had told her that they were the girls who other girls wanted to be. Those girls were jealous of them and they had to keep giving them reasons to be jealous. What better way than by dating a hot senior?

"Are you crazy?" Amber snatched the slip of paper Shawna was holding and replaced it with the one in her hand. "You can give that name back to Mindy. Unless you want it for yourself."

It was on the tip of Shawna's tongue to say that, like Celia, she was going to put back the name Amber had already selected for her. It was Dennis Donahue, North Ridge High's star quarterback. It wasn't that she didn't think Dennis was a catch, but she liked going out with Connor.

"I'm keeping Charlie for myself," Amber said. "Celia might be crazy enough to give him up, but I'm not. She'll realize her mistake Friday night at the dance when she sees us with our hot seniors. Don't you think so?"

Amber was giving her *the look* and Shawna knew what that meant. It meant Amber expected her to agree with her.

Because if she didn't, she would think she was siding with Celia instead of with her.

The last thing Shawna wanted was to get on Amber's bad side.

"*Huge* mistake," Shawna agreed, nodding. "She's going to be *so* jealous of us! You with Charlie and me with Dennis."

"I can't wait to see the look on Charlie's face the night of the Christmas dance when he finds out *I'm* his Secret Santa!" Amber exclaimed.

Chapter Four

The smell of formaldehyde was thick in the air when Celia arrived for Anatomy and Physiology class. At the front of the classroom, Mr. Seleski was peeling away layers of plastic that were covering a row of metal trays filled with gray lumps. She knew those gray lumps were the pigs that they would soon be dissecting. Ugh!

She hurried to the back of the classroom and took her seat next to her lab partner, Freddy Keenan.

"Hey, Freddy."

Freddy looked up from *The X-Files* novel he was reading and gave her a nod before ducking his head back in his book.

Celia liked Freddy, but he hardly ever talked to her! Like today, he always had his nose buried in a book or was too busy taking notes to talk with her. Some of the other lab partners joked and fooled around with each other, but not Freddy. He was always all business. They'd been lab partners since September and she felt like she hardly knew him!

"So what do you think of this whole Secret Santa thing?" Celia asked, taking out her notebook.

Freddy shrugged, not answering.

"You must have an opinion."

Freddy closed his book and pushed his glasses up his nose. "I really don't."

"All right, class," Mr. Seleski announced. "Send someone up to retrieve your specimen."

At those words, Celia instantly turned pale and her stomach began doing flip-flops. "I don't think I can do this," she whispered to Freddy in a panic. Looking around the lab, she was relieved to see that she wasn't the only one freaking out. Some of her other female classmates looked like they were going to lose their lunch, too.

"Don't worry," Freddy said, "you can be my assistant. The way a nurse assists a doctor. I'll do all the cutting. You can hand me the instruments, take notes, and make little flags for the pushpins so I can label everything. How does that sound?"

A smile washed over Celia's face. "That sounds great!"

Freddy smiled back. "Then we're all set!"

True to his word, Freddy did all the cutting and poking around inside. And he didn't do anything stupid like wave pig organs in her face the way some of the other guys were doing to their lab partners. Through most of the period there was a lot of shrieking and squealing and eeewing, but finally it was over.

After class ended, Celia walked with Freddy to his locker. "Sorry for being such a girl."

"Don't worry about it."

"I know the pig is dead, but I can't help feeling sorry for it. When it was on the farm, I'm sure it didn't think it was one day going to be poked and prodded by a bunch of high school sophomores."

"No, it probably thought it was going to wind up in a supermarket as a slab of bacon, a side of sausage, and a rack of barbecued ribs."

Celia giggled. "I'll type up all our notes and email them to you later tonight, okay?"

"Sure."

Celia caught sight of Amber and Shawna headed her way. Knowing they would ignore Freddy because that's what they always did when she was talking to someone they weren't friends with, she quickly rushed away. She didn't want to subject him to their rude behavior, not after he'd been so nice to her today. "See you tomorrow, Freddy."

Froggy watched Celia disappear down the crowded hallway. She turned around and gave him a wave, then joined Amber and Shawna, who didn't even look in his direction. Why would they? To them, he didn't exist. He was the Invisible Man.

He slipped a hand into his pocket and pulled out the slip of paper he'd picked from Mindy Yee's Secret Santa bag.

The name on the slip was Celia's.

He still couldn't believe his luck.

He'd been crushing on Celia since September and now he was her Secret Santa!

He could still remember the very first time

he'd seen her. It had been the first day of classes and he'd been in homeroom. The bell had rung and everyone was in their seats when there was a knock on the classroom door. When it opened, in walked the most beautiful girl he'd ever seen. She looked like one of the girls from *Laguna Beach* or *The Hills*. All golden and glowing. Mrs. Harrison had taken her paperwork and then introduced her to the class.

Froggy was instantly smitten. All he wanted to do was rush up to her, welcome her to North Ridge High, tell her his name, and ask if she needed any help finding her classes. But before he could do any of that, one of the jocks — in this case, Martin "Moose" Novak, who was on the wrestling team — moved in for the kill and Froggy lost his opportunity.

Story of his life.

Although, seriously, if Moose hadn't made the first move, would he have?

Highly doubtful.

Guys like him didn't register with girls like Celia so why subject himself to the rejection?

The next time he saw Celia was later that day in Anatomy and Physiology class. He couldn't believe it when he and Celia were assigned to be lab partners. He kept wanting to pinch himself to make sure he wasn't dreaming.

As they took their seats next to each other, she gave him a smile — a *real* smile, not a phony one like when you have to smile at someone because you have no choice and you're stuck with them. Her whole face had lit up while she was smiling — and said hello, but he had barely been able to say hello back. He was so nervous! He knew this was his chance to become friends with her, but he didn't know what to say.

So after saying hello, he pulled out the latest *Buffy the Vampire Slayer* novel he was reading while Mr. Seleski finished assigning the rest of the class to their seats.

It was a pattern that he would repeat day after day after day.

She would always give him a smile and a hello, asking how he was, and he would barely be able to say hello back. This was his chance to become friends with her but he never knew what to say! So he kept their conversations short and always had his nose buried in a book although he was never able to concentrate on what he was reading. He was always peeking out at her from the corner of his eye.

Unlike most of the pretty and popular girls at North Ridge High, Celia was different.

She was *nice*.

Froggy knew that firsthand because unlike everyone else at North Ridge High, she called him by his real name, the way his teachers did, and not his nickname. Nor did she ask him why everyone called him Froggy, which gave her extra bonus points.

She was also totally unaware of what a knock-out she was. Guys were always doing a double take when she walked down the hallways, but Celia was oblivious to their stares. And she didn't use her looks to get what she wanted the way a lot of pretty girls often did.

She was just Celia.

She didn't think she was better than anyone else at North Ridge High. She didn't cut in front of lines. She said please and thank you. She didn't whisper nasty comments behind people's backs.

But — and this was a BIG but — she was friends with Amber and Shawna.

That he couldn't figure out. How had she hooked up with them? They were so *nasty*. Well, Shawna was more nasty-lite while Amber was nasty-supreme.

That friendship with Amber and Shawna put Celia in a whole other social stratosphere.

There was no way she would be friends with him.

And no way she would even go out with him.

But he wanted to ask her out.

He *so* wanted to!

Froggy stared at the slip of paper still in his hand. He didn't know how he was going to do it, but being Celia's Secret Santa was his chance to let her know he had feelings for her and he wasn't going to blow it.

Lily Norris was on a mission.

To learn everything she could about Connor Hughes so she could be a great Secret Santa to him.

At least she'd chosen someone who had a girlfriend. That way there'd be no thoughts of romance the night of the Christmas dance. Besides, she'd have to be crazy to make a move on Connor. The last thing she wanted to do was get on Shawna's bad side. Christmas catfight anyone? She wouldn't be surprised if Shawna had tattooed PERSONAL PROPERTY OF SHAWNA

WESTON somewhere on Connor's bod, although lately the two weren't together as often as they used to be when they first started dating. Trouble in paradise maybe?

Lily slid her books under the counter of the school library as she took her place behind the front desk. She worked at the library part-time three days a week to make extra spending money. Unlike Amber Davenport, she didn't have a super-rich daddy who gave her credit cards with no spending limit. Her dad was a self-employed carpenter who relied on word of mouth when it came to his jobs. Working at the library was the perfect job because when she wasn't busy checking out books or putting them back on the shelves, she could tackle her own assignments.

She could see Connor sitting across the library, a bunch of textbooks spread out before him, chewing on the eraser of his pencil. He looked deep in thought. Maybe she should go over and ask if he needed some help. That would start a conversation. Even though they had a few classes together, she didn't know much about him. Maybe if they talked, she could learn some things that would help when she started leaving presents for him.

A loud thump startled Lily from her thoughts, and she tore her eyes away from Connor as Mindy Yee dropped a huge chemistry book in front of her.

"I need to take out this book," Mindy said, handing Lily her school ID card.

Lily reached for the scanner wand and waved it across Mindy's card.

"I saw you checking out Connor Hughes," Mindy said knowingly.

"I wasn't checking him out," Lily said.

"Yes, you were. I have eyes. I saw!"

"Slow day for gossip, Mindy?" The last thing Lily wanted was Mindy spreading rumors about her and Connor. Wouldn't Shawna love to hear that? "In case you haven't heard, I'm taking a break from romance." She shoved the chemistry book at her. "Here you go."

"When did you start working here? This is the first time I've seen you behind the desk."

"Right after Thanksgiving."

"Making some extra money for Christmas?"

"Not everyone has a daddy who can give them their own credit cards." The words slipped out before Lily could stop herself and Mindy instantly pounced.

"Meow! Is that a dig at someone in particular?" she asked, her almond-shaped eyes narrowing with glee. "There aren't a lot of girls who have their own credit cards. Amber Davenport is one. Rhianna Ziggler is another. Let's see, who else? Kitty O'Shay and Leslie Finnegan also have their own credit cards."

Over the years, Lily had learned that the best way to deal with Mindy was to neither confirm nor deny anything. Because no matter what you said, Mindy would twist it around. "It amazes me how you always know everything about everybody, Mindy. Is there anything else I can help you with?"

Mindy took another look at Connor. "I wouldn't blame you if you were interested in him. He's definitely a hottie."

"I'm not interested in him." Lily pointed to her chest. "Broken heart? Remember?"

Mindy turned back to Lily, her red lips twitching. "Oh, that's right. I forgot. It must really hurt seeing Jason and Sonia together."

With her pale complexion, red lips, and long, straight, jet-black hair, Mindy sometimes reminded Lily of a vampire. Which she was in a way, always sucking up gossip. It was the tip of Lily's tongue to call her Vampira and see what she said. Instead, Lily only shrugged. "I'm dealing with it."

Mindy leaned across the front desk. "But isn't it driving you crazy that even though they're supposed to be studying, they're not? And right under your nose. It's like they're rubbing it in!"

"What are you talking about?"

"Didn't you know?" Mindy smiled slyly, pointing with a finger. "Jason and Sonia are in the back studying together, but I don't think they've even cracked open a single book!"

Lily followed Mindy's pointing finger. How had she missed seeing them? Jason and Sonia were sitting at a table in the farthest corner of the library. Even though books were spread out around them, they weren't focusing on them. Their chairs were pushed close together, and they were staring into each other's eyes, looking all lovey-dovey.

Barf!!!

Lily knew Mindy expected her to make some sort of nasty remark, but she wasn't going to. If she did, Mindy would make sure Jason and Sonia found out about it. Instead, she gave Mindy a sweet smile. "Anything else I can help you with?"

Mindy slipped the chemistry book into her designer shoulder bag, clearly bummed that Lily wasn't going to do or say anything. "No."

"Guess I'll see you around," Lily said, turning her back on Mindy and loading a cart with books that needed to be reshelved.

When Lily turned back around, Mindy was gone.

And so was Connor.

Rats!

She hadn't had a chance to talk to him and who knew when their paths would cross again? How was she going to figure out his likes and dislikes?

Then the lightbulb went on over Lily's head as she stared at the computer in front of her. All the info she need to know about Connor was right at her fingertips! All she had to do was type Connor's name into the library computer and she'd be able to pull up a list of all the books he had recently checked out! Now she would be able to be the best Secret Santa ever!

Lily's fingers zipped over the keyboard and one minute later the list was on the screen. She studied it closely. Over the last few weeks, Connor had checked out books on car restoration, karate, horror movies, cooking with nuts, Sudoku, and the history of disco.

Lily pressed a button to print out the list. As she did, she stared across the library at Jason and Sonia. She didn't know how it was possible, but somehow, their chairs were pushed even closer together. *Why don't you just sit in his lap?* she thought darkly. *You almost are!* Sonia was smiling at Jason, twirling her fingers through his brown curly hair.

The ache that had been in Lily's heart since Jason broke up with her in late August flared up. The pain wasn't as sharp as it used to be — now it was only a dull ache — but it was still there.

He's a jerk, he's a jerk, he's a jerk, she kept repeating to herself. Sonia was more than welcome to Jason. If he had cheated on her, then who's to say he wouldn't eventually cheat on Sonia, too?

Good riddance!

But it still hurt seeing him with another girl . . .

*   *   *

Outside North Ridge High, Connor Hughes was battling the wind as he pulled a stack of library books out of his backpack. It was wicked cold and he'd forgotten to bring his gloves, so his hands were freezing. Luckily, Simon Larson pulled up in his car, flipping open the passenger door. Connor jumped into the car's toasty warm interior and instantly started blowing on his hands.

"Man, it's nasty out there!" he exclaimed.

"They say we're supposed to get snow this week. Who knows? Maybe we'll have a white Christmas!"

Connor pulled down the mirrored visor above his head and ran his fingers through his wavy black hair, trying to repair the damage the wind had done. His hair was getting too long and he knew he needed to get a haircut before Friday night's dance. His cheeks were cherry red from the cold and his blue eyes sparkled.

"You still look pretty," Simon teased, his own blue eyes glinting with mischief.

"Don't be a wise guy," Connor warned. "Otherwise I won't give you those books I checked out for you this morning."

"Thanks," Simon said, stopping for a red

light. He turned on the radio and the sounds of "Grandma Got Run Over by a Reindeer" filled the car. His dark blond head began bobbing with the music. "I really appreciate it. Did you get everything?"

Connor flipped through the stack of books in his hands. "*Karate 101, Nutty Desserts, Horror Movies to Watch with Your Eyes Closed*, and *The History of Disco*."

"It seems like I have a paper due for every single one of my teachers."

"I don't know how much longer I can keep doing this," Connor said, tossing the books into the backseat. "There's a limit to the number of books I can check out, and all I've been doing the last couple of weeks is checking out books for you. I've got some term papers coming up and I'm going to need some books for myself. When are you going to pay off your library late fees so you can start checking out books again?"

"Soon, soon."

"You still haven't returned the last batch of books I checked out for you and they're due this Friday," Connor reminded. "If you don't return those books then I'm not going to be able to check out any books for you *or* me!"

"Don't worry. Chill out. As soon as I get my next paycheck from Mr. DelMonaco at the pizza parlor I'll pay off the late fees. And I'm going to return the books tomorrow. I promise." The red light turned green and Simon started driving again. "So did you pick someone good for the Secret Santa exchange?"

"I'm not saying."

"You're not even going to give me a hint?" Simon asked, disappointed. "Is it a girl? A hot girl?"

Connor shook his head. "Nope. You'll just have to wait until the night of the Christmas dance to see whose name I picked. How about you? Who'd you pick?"

"Uh-uh," Simon said. "If you're not telling then I'm not telling. You're also going to have to wait and see."

Chapter Five

Noelle loved decorating for Christmas.

The one thing she *didn't* love, though, was lugging boxes filled with Christmas decorations out of her garage.

Which was exactly what she was doing after school.

She'd come home to find a note waiting from her mother, asking her to take the boxes of Christmas decorations out of the garage. Noelle had groaned while reading the note. There had to be at least twenty-five or thirty boxes in the garage, if not more. Her whole afternoon was ruined.

It wasn't like she had made plans. But she wanted to start thinking of what she could leave Charlie as his first Secret Santa gift. She could probably think about it while she was carrying boxes, but she knew once she started opening them up and started decorating, she was going to be more focused on thoughts of Christmas than on Charlie.

Well, she had no choice. When her mother told her to do something, she expected it to get done.

She knew carrying the boxes was going to be hot, sweaty work so she went up to her bedroom and changed into her raggiest pair of jeans and oldest sweatshirt. Then she slipped on an ancient pair of Uggs that used to belong to her mother and pulled her hair into a ponytail. Rather than wear her bulky overcoat, she slipped on her father's neon green down-filled vest and headed back outside to the garage.

Where to begin? she wondered, staring at the array of labeled boxes. There were boxes labeled ANGELS, OUTDOOR CHRISTMAS LIGHTS, INDOOR CHRISTMAS LIGHTS, REINDEER, SANTAS, ELVES, SNOWMEN, TINSEL, ORNAMENTS.

The easiest thing to do was to just start carrying boxes. The outdoor decorations she'd pile on the porch and the indoor decorations she'd bring inside.

But there were so many boxes!

Knowing the sooner she got started, the sooner she would finish, Noelle gave a sigh and started carrying. Some of the boxes were light as a feather, but others were quite heavy. After thirty minutes, drops of sweat were trickling down the sides of her forehead and her hands were all dirty and grimy. She was staggering out of the garage with one of the next-to-last boxes when she saw Charlie pull up into his driveway in his car.

Catching sight of him, Noelle almost dropped the box she was carrying, but caught herself in time. After leaving the box on the front porch, she raced inside and checked herself out in the hallway mirror. She wasn't surprised by what she saw. She looked a mess! There was a sheen of sweat on her face, along with smears of dust on her forehead and cheeks. Her ponytail was limp, and the clothes she was wearing made her look like a huge fashion don't.

Well, there wasn't much she could do, but at least she'd try.

She raced to the downstairs bathroom and washed her hands, then once they were clean tossed some water on her face, scrubbing away at the smudges, and blotted it dry. Pulling her hair out of its ponytail, she ran a brush through it, fluffing it out over her shoulders. Finally, she took off the neon green vest and pulled up the sleeves of her sweatshirt.

Before leaving the house, she gave herself another look in the hallway mirror.

Not great, but better than before.

It was the best she could do on such short notice.

Back outside, Charlie and Ryan were emptying out the trunk of the car. She could see they were carrying bags of groceries. Mrs. Grant, who worked full-time in Manhattan as a legal secretary, must have asked them to stop at the supermarket.

"Need any help?" she called out.

Charlie slammed down the lid of the trunk with one hand and headed inside. "Nah, we're all set."

"How about you?" Ryan asked, walking over to Noelle's house. "I saw you carrying some boxes. Need some help?"

This was a new side of Ryan. Growing up together, he had pretty much been her nemesis. The bratty brother she never had who was always looking to make her life miserable. When they were younger he would kidnap her dolls and hold them for ransom. When Lily would come over for tea parties in her backyard, he'd always crash them, pretending he was King Kong or Godzilla and throwing over the table, stomping on her dishes and cups, while roaring like the monster he was pretending to be. At school he would slip spiders into her lunch box or worms down her back, laughing hysterically when she would freak out. During the summers, he'd squirt her with the hose while watering the front lawn or toss her into the pool in his backyard. With all her clothes on.

But in the last two years Ryan had stopped teasing and tormenting her. In the beginning, she'd been suspicious, wondering if it was all part of some elaborate scheme meant to catch her off guard before he lowered the boom.

But it hadn't.

Ryan had finally grown up.

The last box in the garage was the Christmas tree. It was too big and bulky for her to carry out by herself. Once it was inside and assembled, she could start decorating it and get rid of some of the other boxes.

"Some help would be great," she said. "Thanks."

"Let me just bring this bag inside and I'll be right over."

Whenever Noelle thought of Ryan and Charlie, she thought of famous brothers. Like Nick and Drew Lachey. Nick and Aaron Carter. Matt Dillon and Kevin Dillon. Rob Lowe and Chad Lowe. She didn't know why, but the older brother was always the better-looking of the two, and the younger brother was always the pale imitation. It was the same with Charlie and Ryan.

Ryan's hair was blond like Charlie's, but it wasn't light blond. It was more of a dirty blond. Unlike Charlie, Ryan's hair was never neatly combed. It was always a tousled mess that looked like it needed to be cut. His eyes were green but not a bright, shiny, emerald green like Charlie's. More of a softer, paler sea green. Charlie's clothes always looked liked they came right off the pages of an Abercrombie & Fitch catalog while Ryan shopped exclusively at Old Navy, always wearing T-shirts, plaid shirts, and cargo pants that were wrinkly and screamed to be ironed.

Ten minutes later, Noelle and Ryan were

carrying the Christmas tree into the house. They left it in the hallway outside the living room, while Noelle started moving the love seat that was in front of the living room window.

"Wow!" Ryan whistled. "Look at all these boxes. Are they all filled with Christmas decorations?"

"My mom is a Christmas freak," Noelle explained. "She likes decorating every room in the house. And she lives for after-Christmas sales. The number of boxes grows each year."

"How come you guys don't have a real Christmas tree?" Ryan asked as he opened the box holding the pieces of the tree. He took out the stand and slipped a long green pole down the hole in its center.

"My dad's allergic to pine so we can't have one."

"Oh."

Noelle started helping Ryan add the snow-covered branches. Within minutes a lush tree was standing before them.

"Now for the fun part!" Ryan exclaimed, rubbing his hands together.

"You don't have to stay and help. I can handle the rest myself."

"Are you kidding? I love decorating Christmas trees. Just tell me what you want me to do."

Noelle shrugged and pointed to a pile of boxes. "You can start with those if you want."

Ryan started peeking in boxes. "Hey, I remember this!" He held up a snowman made of cotton balls and twigs. "You made this in the fourth grade."

Noelle looked up from the knotted string of Christmas tree lights that she was trying to unravel. "We made those in Mrs. Fleishman's Art class. You dabbed your snowman with red dots. You said he was a snowman soldier who'd been in battle and the red dots were blood."

"My mom still has it," Ryan said, hanging the snowman on a bottom branch.

"She hangs it on the back of your tree. Don't think I haven't noticed."

Ryan held up a Styrofoam cup covered with bits of colored tissue paper and a yellow pipe-cleaner hook. "What's this supposed to be?"

"A Christmas bell! Don't you remember? We made those in third grade."

"I was out sick with the chicken pox that December. I must have missed the class."

Noelle laughed. "That's right! When I brought

over your homework one day, your face was covered with pink calamine lotion and your mom had covered your hands with white tube socks so you couldn't scratch yourself."

Noelle finally unraveled the tangled Christmas lights and began wrapping them around the branches of the tree. "So what's new with Charlie?" she asked, hoping her question sounded casual.

"What do you mean?

"Is he excited about graduating this year?" She finished wrapping the lights and plugged them in. Instantly, the bright-colored lights began blinking on and off, on and off.

"I guess," Ryan said.

"Does he know where he's going to college?" she asked as she began hanging ornaments on the tree.

"He's been filling out a lot of applications. He says he wants to go out of state."

Noelle gasped, but quickly covered it up with a cough so Ryan wouldn't get suspicious.

Go out of state? Charlie wanted to attend college out of state? But if he did that, she'd never see him except during summers and when he was home for the holidays. And what if he decided to take summer classes? Or *not* come home for the holidays? What if he met a girl at college and he went home to her family? No!!!

"Is he dating anyone new?"

Ryan rolled his eyes as he began draping silver tinsel on the tree. "Who knows? Girls call our house all the time. Their voices all sound alike to me. You know Charlie. It seems like every week he has a new girlfriend."

That was so not what she wanted to hear!

"But he's not serious about anyone, is he?"

"Nah, I don't think so." Ryan looked away from the glass ornament he'd just hung. It was a midnight blue ball sprinkled with gold glitter. "Why so many questions about Charlie?"

"I haven't seen him in a while," Noelle said as she hung an ornament shaped like an icicle and then added one shaped like a snowflake. "I was just wondering what was new with him."

"How about asking what's new with me?"

"I see you every day. What could be new with you?"

"I'm heading up the school's Toys for Tots program this year. You're familiar with it, right?"

Noelle nodded as she added a wooden soldier to the tree. "Sure. They collect toys for needy kids."

"Tomorrow afternoon I'm going to be shopping for toys and then I'm going to have to wrap them. Want to help out? I could use any many hands as possible."

"Okay."

"Maybe you might want to mention it to Lily."

"Sure. Are you asking Charlie?"

"I already did, but he's too busy. He's playing Scrooge in the school Christmas play and he has rehearsal tomorrow."

If she'd known Charlie was going to be in the Christmas play, she would have auditioned for a part herself!

Ryan checked the time on his watch. "I better be getting home. I've still got homework to tackle, and my mom and I are doing some Christmas shopping at the mall tonight." He took a step back and admired the decorated tree. "Not bad. There are few spots that still need to be filled in, but looking good, don't you think?"

Noelle walked over to Ryan and gazed at the tree. "I agree."

"It's just missing one thing."

"What's that?"

Ryan gazed around at the boxes before finally finding the one he was searching for. Lifting off the lid, he pushed aside sheets of tissue paper and removed a Christmas angel. She was wearing a light blue gown and her wings were silver. Ryan stood on his tiptoes and placed her on top of the tree. Then he took a step back.

"The finishing touch," he said. "What do you think?"

"Perfect!" Noelle exclaimed. "Absolutely perfect!"

Chapter Six

"My dress for the Christmas dance needs to be *perfect*!" Amber exclaimed to Shawna. "Absolutely perfect!"

Amber and Shawna were standing in Amber's walk-in closet. Surrounding them were racks of dresses, sweaters, skirts, tops, jackets, jeans, shoes, and sneakers. It was like being in a mini–department store!

"These are what I've narrowed my choices down to," Amber explained as she removed a bunch of dresses off a rack. "We could go sparkly." She held up a sequined wool jersey in silver, then a white silk organza shift with black embroidered swirl details, and a yellow lace minidress.

"Those are definitely eye-catching," Shawna said, knowing that Amber had bought all the dresses during September's Fashion Week. Amber's mother, Yvonne, worked as a writer for a fashion magazine and always had a seat at all the shows. Often Amber got to go with her mother and once or twice had even invited Shawna to come along.

"Or I could go with a floral look," Amber said, showing Shawna a peach baby doll dress decorated with tiny rosebuds and then a creamy petal-like scalloped dress.

"Those are nice, too," Shawna offered.

"Or I can go va-va-va-voom with something low cut." Amber held up a violet dress and an emerald green dress, both with plunging necklines. "I think I'm leaning toward the low cut, even though my mother told me she might be able to bring home a few new dresses before Friday. Something low cut will definitely get Charlie's attention, don't you think?"

"He won't be able to take his eyes off you," Shawna said. "Speaking of Charlie, do know what you're going to buy him as his first Secret Santa gift? I've been racking my brain trying to figure out one for Dennis."

Amber stopped hanging the dresses she was putting back. "You're not serious, are you? You're crazy if you buy him more than one gift. Girls don't spend money on guys — guys spend money on girls!"

"Does that mean you're not going to be leaving Charlie Secret Santa gifts all week?"

"That's right," Amber said, turning off the lights in her closet and heading back out into the bedroom, which was Amber's favorite color, pink. From the walls to the rug to the bedspread, pink was the dominant color.

"In fact, the only gift Charlie will be getting from me will be a kiss under the mistletoe at the Christmas dance."

"But we're supposed to buy at least one gift," Shawna argued.

"My gift to Charlie will be looking gorgeous!" Amber proclaimed, staring at herself in the mirror over her dresser and fluffing out her hair.

"I've already gotten a gift from my Secret Santa," Shawna confessed. "It was waiting for me when I got home from school."

"What was it?"

"A tube of peppermint-flavored lip gloss," Shawna said, reaching into her shoulder bag and showing it to Amber.

There had also been a note, but Shawna didn't

81

want to tell Amber what the note said. She didn't know what to make of it yet. Shawna could still remember every last word of the note: *There's nothing I love more than a Christmas kiss. Especially one that tastes like a candy cane!*

Was her Secret Santa someone who had a crush on her? He definitely wanted a Christmas kiss and she'd be happy to give him one . . . *if* he was worth it. She'd have to figure out how she was going to handle things on Friday night.

"A tube of lip gloss?" Amber sneered, snatching the tube out of Shawna's hand and turning it over before handing it back. "That's what your Secret Santa left you? Talk about cheap!"

"Huh?"

"That lip gloss can be bought in any drugstore."

"So?"

"I wouldn't be caught dead wearing it!"

"That's right, I forgot," Shawna said, trying not to sound sarcastic and failing. "You only buy your makeup at department stores."

"You get what you pay for," Amber sniffed.

Shawna disagreed. When she did wear makeup, she wore Revlon and Cover Girl and always liked the results.

"You're not the only one who got a gift from their Secret Santa," Amber announced. "I did too!"

"What'd you get? What'd you get?" Shawna asked excitedly.

Amber reached into a dresser drawer and pulled out a beautiful silk scarf in a black-and-white polka-dot pattern, waving it in the air.

Shawna's eyes bugged out when she saw the scarf. "That must have cost more than we're allowed to spend!"

The rules of the Secret Santa exchange said that store-bought gifts couldn't exceed more than twenty dollars. Multiple gifts were fine, and gifts could be homemade, but there was a ceiling on how much could be spent. Of course, nothing in the rules said you could get in trouble for overspending. Which was what Amber's Secret Santa had obviously done!

Amber shrugged. "What can I say? I'm worth it!" She waved the scarf in Shawna's face and it was all Shawna could do not to tear it out of Amber's hands. She couldn't stand it when Amber was gloating. "Obviously my Secret Santa thinks I'm worth more than yours thinks you're worth!"

* ★ * ★ *

"That will be ten dollars," Froggy said, handing over a white box of cupcakes.

It was early evening, and Froggy was working as a cashier at Icing on the Cake, a bakery/coffeehouse. The store was super busy with tons of Christmas shoppers coming in for cocoa, hot apple cider, coffee, cupcakes, as well as other yummy homemade desserts.

Froggy had been working at the bakery part-time since early June. He liked the job because his boss, Gloria, was cool and never had a problem if he needed to change his hours because he had a test to study for or a paper to write. And the coffeehouse was such a warm, cozy place. There were tons of oversized couches and arm-chairs filled with throw pillows, the walls were painted a sunshiny yellow, and the coffee tables were piled with the latest magazines and newspapers. There was always the *tap-tap-tapping* of people working on their laptops and music always filled the air. Gloria usually preferred to play something mellow and easy listening, although sometimes he and his coworker, Jake Morrisey, would be able to slip in a more modern CD like Scissor Sisters or The Killers.

Tonight Gloria had chosen a Christmas CD, and "Rudolph the Red-Nosed Reindeer" was playing.

After finishing with his customer, Froggy popped into the kitchen, where he knew Jake was working. When he walked in, Jake looked up from the chocolate cupcakes he was icing with white frosting. He held one out to Froggy. "Want one?"

One of the perks of working at Icing on the Cake was all the cupcakes he could eat. That fringe benefit had quickly worn off after two weeks of stuffing his face. Now Froggy couldn't even stand looking at them.

"I'll pass."

Jake placed it on a tray with the other cupcakes he had already frosted. "Hey, I got a question for you."

"Shoot."

"I picked a girl to be a Secret Santa for. Any ideas on what I should buy her?"

"Do you know anything about her?"

Jake shrugged. "Not a thing."

"If you don't know much about her, you can't go wrong with candy or flowers. That's a good start."

"Thanks, man. You always have the answers for me."

Froggy and Jake had become friends from working together at Icing on the Cake. Like Froggy, Jake was low man on the North Ridge High social ladder, but that was by choice. Jake wasn't a nerd but a bad boy. With his black leather jacket, motorcycle, and endless afternoons spent in detention, Jake pretty much did as he pleased. He wasn't flunking out, but his grades could be better and Froggy sometimes helped him with his studying.

They had bonded Froggy's first week on the job. Froggy hadn't gotten a grip on how to use an icing bag, so when he decorated cakes his little swirls and rosebuds looked like big blobs.

"Here, let me show you how to do it," Jake had said, taking the bag out of his hand. "Think of it like writing in script." He demonstrated. "See?" He handed over the bag. "Now you try."

Froggy kept Jake's comments in mind and tried again. As he created a swirl around the bottom of a cake, he noticed the T-shirt Jake was wearing. "You like Duran Duran?"

"One of the best bands of the eighties. I saw them last summer in concert at Jones Beach."

"Me too!"

Within seconds Froggy and Jake were talking about their favorite bands and the next week they were exchanging CDs and telling each other about groups the other one hadn't heard of.

"What brings you back here?" Jake asked. "Things quiet down out front?"

Froggy looked over his shoulder. "For the moment. But I'm sure it's going to get busy again."

"What'd you need?"

Froggy felt shy asking the question but who else could he ask? So he plunged right in. "What do you do when you like a girl, but you don't know how to tell her?"

Jake shrugged. "I don't know. I've never had that problem."

"Duh! No kidding," Froggy said. "You're Mr. Irresistible."

It was true. Girls not only from North Ridge High but also some of the other local high schools were constantly coming to the bakery and staying in their seats long after they'd eaten their cupcakes or finished their hot drinks. When Jake was behind the counter, they took an extra long time to make up their mind when ordering and then they'd flirt and talk with him while waiting for their order. Jake would usually flirt back because it meant he'd get a tip. And sometimes even a phone number!

"You got a crush on someone?" Jake asked.

Froggy nodded. He didn't know why it was so hard to say Celia's name out loud. David was his best friend and even he didn't have a clue that he was crushing on Celia. Maybe it was because he was afraid if he told other people, they would tell him that he was crazy. That there was no way a pretty, popular girl like Celia would go for a guy like him.

"Who is she? Wanna give me a clue?"

"It's Celia Armstrong," Froggy whispered, almost as if he was afraid of being overheard.

"Celia Armstrong?" Jake mused. Then his face lit up. "You mean Beach Girl!"

"Yes," Froggy said. "Beach Girl." He felt Celia's nickname made her even more unobtainable because every guy he knew dreamed of going out with a California beach girl and his school only had one. What were the chance that *he* would be able to go out with her?

Slim to none!

"She's in my Art class," Jake said. "You like her?"

Froggy blushed. "Yes."

Jake shrugged. "So what's the problem? Tell her."

"I can't."

"Then she's never going to know how you feel about her."

Froggy worked up his courage. "I thought maybe *you* could help me do that."

"Me? How?"

"Not only are you in the same Art class, but your locker is right next to hers. Maybe you could start talking to her? Find out her likes and dislikes and then tell me what you find out? I'm her Secret Santa. I can use what you find out to buy her presents. I don't know anything about her."

Jake shook his head. "I'm not into playing Cupid. Sorry. Find someone else."

Those were *not* the words Froggy had been expecting to hear!

"Jake, you owe me!" he shouted.

Jake looked at Froggy in stunned surprise, never before having seen him lose his temper. Froggy, himself, was also a bit surprised at his outburst, but he was mad. He needed Jake's help!

"Haven't I helped you study for tests? Haven't I taken shifts for you at the last minute when you couldn't make it to work? And didn't I help you fill out your college applications last week?"

"That was a waste of paper and pen," Jake snorted, going back to his cupcakes.

"There's more to life than just listening to music and riding your motorcycle, Jake. Friends help each other out. I thought you were my friend, but I guess I was wrong."

"Okay, okay! Enough with the guilt. I'll do it!" Jake pointed the knife he was using to frost with at Froggy. "I'll see what I can find out. But then we're squared. Deal?"

"Deal!"

The smell of vanilla was thick in Noelle's kitchen. She and Lily were in the midst of making a batch of chocolate chip cookies. They had decided the cookies would be their first Secret Santa gifts to

Charlie and Connor. What guy could resist a batch of ooey-gooey chocolate chip cookies?

The TV on the counter was also on, tuned in to Noelle's favorite Christmas movie, *It's a Wonderful Life*. She had lost count of the number of times she had seen it over the years, but no matter how many times she watched it, she always got teary-eyed during certain scenes.

"Guess who I saw this afternoon?" Noelle said as she measured out two cups of flour.

"Who?" Lily asked while she measured out white sugar and brown sugar.

"Charlie!"

"And?"

"And what?"

"You saw him and . . ."

"That's it," Noelle said, mixing the flour with baking soda and salt in a large bowl.

Lily sighed. "Noelle, I saw Charlie Grant today too. That doesn't mean we're going to be living happily ever after."

"What are you saying?"

Lily put a stick of butter in the microwave and left it in for a minute so it would melt. Then she stirred it into the sugar and added vanilla extract. "You're going to need to start getting more proactive. If you want Charlie, you're going to have to go after him."

"What do you think I'm going to be doing this week with my Secret Santa gifts?" she asked, nibbling on a handful of chocolate chips.

"But you're *not* his Secret Santa," Lily reminded. "You're Ryan's. Shouldn't you be focusing on him?"

"Being Ryan's Secret Santa is the last thing on my mind," Noelle said. "I have to focus on Charlie! I'll probably buy Ryan a gift and give it to him the night of the Christmas dance."

"What are you going to get him?" Lily asked as she cracked an egg and mixed it in with the sugar and butter before adding another. Then she started adding in the flour mixture from Noelle's bowl. When it was all mixed in, she added the chocolate chips and began spooning out the dough on a cookie sheet.

"Who knows?" Noelle shrugged as she began spooning out dough on a second cookie sheet. "Ryan's like a brother to me so it shouldn't be too hard."

"Noelle, I don't want to burst your bubble," Lily said. "But —"

"Then don't!" Noelle cut her off.

"But I can't remember the last time Charlie went out with an underclassman. When he was a sophomore, he dated sophomores. When he was a junior, he dated juniors. Now that he's a senior, all he's been dating are seniors. See the pattern?"

"Patterns were made to be broken!" Noelle exclaimed as she slid two cookie sheets into the heated oven. "Operation Secret Santa *is* going to be a success!"

Chapter Seven

The package was waiting on Noelle's front porch.

When she walked out her front door, her foot hit it and it went skittering to the top of the front steps. The sound is what made her look down. When she did, she saw there was a gift-wrapped package.

And it was addressed to her.

The wrapping paper was silver with a red foil bow. The package was tiny and could fit in the palm of her hand. A card was attached with her name on it, but she didn't open it. The card could wait. She was dying to see what was inside the box.

Taking off her mittens, she tore away the wrapping paper and lifted the lid of the box.

Inside, nestled on a bed of white cotton, was a tiny Christmas angel. It was adorable.

Noelle finally opened the note attached to the top of the box and read it: *Every Christmas tree needs a Christmas angel. Merry Xmas! Your Secret Santa.*

Noelle's heart started beating with excitement. Yesterday afternoon Charlie saw her lugging boxes of Christmas decorations out of her garage. When he was taking out the garbage last night, he saw her stringing lights around her porch with her father and positioning Santa and his reindeer on the front lawn. Could the angel be from him? He knew she had been decorating yesterday so it kind of made sense. Like he was sending her a message.

Noelle went back inside and hung the angel on the Christmas tree. It looked perfect nestled among the bright colored balls and tinsel.

Could Charlie really be her Secret Santa? It was too much to hope for! She'd have to discuss it with Lily once she got to school, but before that she had to leave Charlie his own Secret Santa gift.

Making sure no one saw her, she walked over to Charlie's house. She checked the time on her watch. 7:30. Perfect. She knew Charlie didn't usually leave for school until 8:00. She left her box of cookies on his front porch and then raced away.

Celia was at her locker getting her books for her morning classes when she heard a voice call her name.

But it couldn't be?

Could it?

He'd never spoken to her before.

Celia turned around slowly, not believing that the person she hoped to find waiting would be there.

But she was wrong.

He was!

It was Jake!

Celia couldn't find her voice. She was speechless.

Jake Morrisey was standing mere inches away from her. Of course, that wasn't new. Their lockers were side by side and there were days when they were getting their books at the same time. Even when her back was turned to him, she was aware of his presence because of the cologne he wore. It had a light, woodsy scent.

But today was the first time he was talking to her.

How many times had she imagined herself starting a conversation with him? But the words would always get stuck in her throat. No matter how hard she tried, they wouldn't come out. Part of her wondered if it was because she was afraid he wouldn't say anything back. After all, he was a senior and she was a sophomore. Why would he want to bother with her?

Another part of her wondered if it was because she was afraid of Amber. She knew she wouldn't like the idea of her going out with Jake. Not after all her efforts to set her up on dates with North Ridge High's A-list guys. In Amber's book, Jake was *not* boyfriend material. To her, he was a loser.

She'd first noticed Jake in Art class. There was no mistaking him. From the way he looked to the way he acted, dark and moody were the words that instantly came to mind. He was so different from the guys she'd grown up with in California, who all had blond hair and blue eyes.

Jake was the complete opposite. He had shoulder-length brown hair that she wanted to run her fingers through and flashing brown eyes. Often he wore T-shirts with cutoff sleeves that showed off his nicely muscled arms. His jeans were faded and torn, but they clung in all the right places, and he was always wearing motorcycle boots.

Jake had his own style and it stood out.

He did what he wanted when he wanted and didn't answer to anyone.

Of course, that had gotten him into trouble on more than one occasion with his teachers. Many afternoons, on her way to her locker after last class, she'd passed by the detention room and seen Jake arriving.

But she didn't care.

She liked that rebellious side of him.

Maybe it was because deep down, she wished she could be that way herself.

"It's Celia, right?"

Celia nodded, still unable to find her voice.

"You do talk, don't you?"

Celia was so nervous, she dropped the books that were in her hands. They fell to the floor with a loud bang, although it was so noisy in the hallway, with lockers opening and closing and nonstop conversations going on, that nobody noticed.

She bent down to get her books the same time Jake did and their heads smashed together.

"Ow!" she exclaimed.

"So you do talk," Jake said, rubbing his forehead while offering Celia her books.

"I'm usually not such a klutz," she apologized, taking the books from Jake and rubbing her own forehead.

"Are you reading that for English class?" he said, pointing to Celia's copy of Jane Austen's *Pride and Prejudice*.

"Actually, I'm reading it for fun."

Jake made a face. "You're reading it for *fun*?"

Celia nodded. "Last month my English teacher, Mrs. Olivant, assigned us *Emma* to read. I loved it so much, I wanted to read Jane Austen's other books."

"I had Olivant when I was a sophomore. She loves assigning novels. I never read them, though. Either I'd see if there was a movie version or I'd buy the Cliff Notes."

"But that's cheating!" The words slipped out before Celia could stop herself. *Great way to make an impression*, she scolded herself. *Let him think you're Miss Priss!*

Jake gave her a wicked grin. "I like to call it taking a shortcut. So listen, Ceel —"

He called her Ceel! No one had ever called her Ceel. It was like his own special nickname for her.

"I can't remember when we have to turn in that midterm assignment for Art class. It's due January eighteenth, right?"

"Right. How could I forget? January is my least favorite month of the year."

"How come?"

"All the Christmas decorations are down. It gets dark way early. The snow isn't white and fluffy anymore. It's usually all gray and slushy."

"But Valentine's Day is right around the corner," Jake reminded. "That's something to look forward to."

"It is if you have a boyfriend, but I don't." She made sure to drop that little tidbit and waited to see what he would say.

"Who knows?" Jake gave her a wink. "Maybe you'll have one next year."

Celia's breath caught. Was he flirting with her? She studied his face, but she didn't see any secret message or expression that indicated he meant something more than what he'd said. She was so lousy at this! Why hadn't she been paying closer attention when Amber was flirting with guys? She always knew what to do and say to get what she wanted.

"Have you gotten a gift yet from your Secret Santa?" she asked, knowing he had since she'd left his gift earlier.

Jake held up a wrapped package. "I found this waiting in front of my locker this morning, but I haven't opened it up yet."

"How come? I can't resist a wrapped present."

Jake shrugged. "How great can it be? We can't spend a lot of money, and whoever picked me probably doesn't know a thing about me."

"You never know. Come on!" she urged. "Open it up!"

Jake tore away the wrapping paper covered with snowmen, revealing a folded red bandana. Celia had made it herself, using fabric she'd found in her mother's sewing room. She figured Jake could wear it around his head to hold his hair back when he was riding his motorcycle or use it to clean his hands when he was working on the engine.

"Like I don't already own one of these," Jake scoffed, opening his locker and tossing the bandana inside.

Celia was bummed that Jake didn't like her gift. Okay, it hadn't been the most imaginative gift, but at least it had been something. She'd just have to do better with the next one. She wanted to make an impression on Jake!

"Have you bought a gift yet for the person whose name you picked?" Celia asked.

Jake gave Celia a wink and a smile. "I know *exactly* what to buy for the person whose name I picked." The bell for first period rang and he slammed his locker shut. "See you later."

"Later," Celia said, wondering what Jake meant by his wink and feeling even more confused.

Froggy was the first person to arrive for Anatomy and Physiology class. Since no one else was there, he used the opportunity to leave Celia's Secret Santa gift. Because he didn't know anything about her yet, he'd gone the safe route and bought a Christmas card and candy cane. Hopefully by the end of the day, Jake would have some info to share and his next gift would be better.

Soon students began arriving for class, and then Celia was standing in front of her desk.

"Looks like your Secret Santa was here," Froggy said, pointing to the card and candy cane on her seat.

"Did you see who left this?" Celia asked. Before Froggy could answer, she held up a hand. "Wait! Don't tell me. I don't want to know. I want to be kept in suspense." Seconds later, Celia changed her mind. "Tell me!" she begged. "Did you see who left it?"

Froggy shook his head. "I didn't see anyone leave it."

"Bummer," Celia said, slipping into her seat. She opened the card, which had a baby reindeer on it, and showed it to Froggy. "Cute." She broke off a piece of her candy cane and offered it to Froggy. "Want some?"

"No thanks."

"I love when Anatomy and Physiology is our first class of the day," she said, putting a piece of candy cane in her mouth. "That means we can get it over with and I don't have to dread coming in here."

Froggy never dreaded Anatomy and Physiology. It was his favorite class of the day because with the exception of homeroom, which only lasted fifteen minutes, it was the only class he shared with Celia.

He watched from the corner of his eye as Celia sucked on her candy cane. He couldn't help but notice that she had a dreamy expression on her face. She had to be thinking about a guy, but who? He'd give anything to be the guy she was thinking of.

At that moment, Mr. Seleski arrived in the lab. "Okay, class, take out a piece of paper," he announced, dropping his books on his desk and picking up a piece of chalk. He began writing on the blackboard. "Hopefully you all read last night's assignment because we're going to have a pop quiz."

Froggy groaned along with the rest of the class as he took out a sheet of paper and wrote his name on top. Great! First Celia was thinking about another guy and now a surprise quiz. Could his day get any worse?

Lily felt like one of Santa's elves!

She was sitting behind her desk, flipping

through her Algebra II notebook while casually glancing at Connor's desk. He hadn't arrived for class yet, but the cookies she'd made for him were sitting on top of his desk. She'd slipped in before anyone else, left them on his desk, and then slipped out before returning with some other students. From the wrapped gifts sitting on top of other desks, she wasn't the only one who'd done the same thing.

She couldn't wait to see the expression on Connor's face when he saw his present.

The bell for first period rang and the rest of the class began walking in. Shawna entered the room first, looking fab in a black silk dress with a gold star-pattern and black high-heeled boots. Her eyes widened when she saw the wrapped box on Connor's desk. Lily had to admit that she did a great job when it came to wrapping. Last Christmas she had worked at Macy's in the gift wrap department and learned how to wrap a box the right way. Of all the boxes in the room, hers looked the best.

Shawna snatched the box off Connor's desk and gave it a shake. It was all Lily could do not to jump up and tear it out of her hands. She was shaking it so hard, she was going break the cookies! By the time Connor opened it up, he'd be lucky to have a box of crumbs!

Shawna's eyes traveled around the classroom, zeroing in on just the girls, as if trying to figure out who had left Connor's gift. Her gaze would linger for a few seconds and then move on. Watching her, Lily kept expecting laser beams to come shooting out of her eyes. When Shawna's gaze fell on her, Lily tried not to squirm in her seat. Luckily, Shawna spent no more than a second looking at her.

Connor entered the classroom then and Shawna flung the box at him. "Guess who got a present from their Secret Santa?"

Walking behind Connor was a smirking Amber, looking equally fab in a black leather miniskirt, silver-link belt with a jeweled buckle, and violet boatneck top. She took Shawna by the arm and led her to her seat. As they walked by, Lily could hear Amber whisper in Shawna's ear, "Jealous, much?"

Jealous? Shawna was jealous? About what? Lily wondered. She wasn't going after her boyfriend. All she was doing was participating in the Secret Santa game!

She turned her attention back to Connor. He had slid into his seat and was unwrapping her box. Then he lifted the lid and looked inside.

Lily expected him to reach into the box for a cookie and take a huge bite.

But he didn't.

Instead, he made a face of total disgust.

That was the last thing Lily expected him to do. She couldn't understand it. She and Noelle had sampled the cookies last night. They were delicious! The yummy chocolatey smell of the cookies had wafted out of the box even after it was wrapped. What could have gone wrong?

Connor *hated* chocolate chip cookies. He was more of a peanut butter cookie or oatmeal raisin kind of guy.

"Do you want these?" he asked Simon, holding out the box. "I hate chocolate chip cookies."

Never one to turn down free food, Simon snatched the box out of Connor's hands. "Sure!" He began stuffing cookies in his mouth. "Thanks. These taste great! Why couldn't my Secret Santa have left me a box of cookies?"

"What did yours leave you?"

"Soap on a rope! Is my Secret Santa saying I smell?"

"If it's after a track meet, the answer is yes!"

Simon punched Connor in the arm. "Very funny!"

Connor looked in Shawna's direction, but she wouldn't look at him. She kept staring directly at the blackboard. He could tell she was mad, but about what? What had he done wrong? All he'd done was unwrap a gift left by his Secret Santa.

He was tempted to send her a text message, asking if everything was okay, but he knew if he got caught, Mrs. Baxter would confiscate his cell phone. He'd have to talk to her after class. Hopefully she'd tell him what was going on because some days he just couldn't figure her out.

I am not jealous. I am not jealous. I am not jealous.

Shawna kept repeating the words to herself, but there was no escaping the fact.

She *was* jealous!

She knew Connor's Secret Santa was a girl. Only a girl would wrap a package so perfectly and only a girl would make a batch of homemade chocolate chip cookies. Luckily for her, Connor hated chocolate chip cookies.

But that didn't mean the next gift wouldn't be a success.

And if it was, she could be in trouble.

She was already getting the sense that Connor was drifting away from her. He'd been so busy the last couple of weeks with basketball practice, basketball games, studying for classes, and working his part-time job that she barely saw him outside of school. If she meant something to him, wouldn't he make time for her?

She was feeling neglected. And unwanted. She was Shawna Westin! She could go out with any guy at North Ridge High and Connor was the guy she had chosen to go out with. Connor was the guy she had been falling in love with, but Connor was acting like he didn't want her anymore and she resented it.

Big time!

She could still remember the first time he'd asked her out. It had been this summer at the beach and she'd been wearing an adorable pink polka-dot bikini. He'd asked if he could borrow her sunscreen, and after slathering his arms, legs, and chest, he'd asked if she wouldn't mind putting some on his back.

Mind? Why would she mind?! He was a chiseled hunk!

Before she could answer, he had plopped down on her blanket and inched closer to her.

As she'd added the sunscreen to his back, they'd started talking and when she was finished, he asked if he could buy her an ice-cream cone. When they walked to the concession stand, he also asked if she wanted to go to a movie that night.

She instantly accepted, knowing that if Amber had been there, she would have freaked out. When it came to dating, Amber's first rule was never to accept at once. She believed in keeping guys dangling and getting back to them with an answer. But Amber hadn't come with her to the beach that day so Shawna had done what she wanted.

That first date had led to a second date and a third and before she knew it, she was spending the rest of the summer with Connor when she wasn't hanging out with Amber and Celia. That all ended when classes began again in September, but she had been busy, too, adjusting to her new class schedule and after-school activities. Still, she and Connor had made time for each other.

That is, until the last couple of weeks.

What had suddenly changed?

She had never gone chasing after a guy before and she wasn't about to start now.

But that didn't mean she was going to make it easy for Connor's Secret Santa.

She was going to find out who she was.

And then she was going to tell her to back off!

Chapter Eight

"Were the cookies a success?" Noelle asked at lunch as she took a seat next to Lily.

"That depends on who you ask." Lily sighed as she began peeling an orange.

"Huh?"

"Connor hated the cookies, but Simon loved them."

"Simon?"

"Connor hates chocolate chip cookies so he gave them to Simon," Lily explained, popping an orange slice in her mouth.

"Oops!"

"Big oops! I'm going to have to do better with my next gift although there might be a little bit of a problem."

"A problem?"

"Named Shawna."

Noelle started shaking a container of raspberry yogurt. "What's Shawna got to do with this?"

"She didn't seem too happy to see Connor getting a gift from his Secret Santa. I think she was a little jealous. She gave Connor the deep freeze before class, and when he tried talking to her after class ended, she wouldn't."

"Yikes!" Noelle exclaimed, peeling the lid off her yogurt.

"The last thing I need is for her to be coming after me because she thinks I'm after her boyfriend, so I'm going to have be *extremely* careful when I leave Connor his gifts."

"What's going to happen the night of the dance when you reveal yourself?"

"I'll worry about that on Friday. So, how did things go with *your* cookies?"

"I'm not sure," Noelle said, spooning into her yogurt. "I left them on his doorstep along with a note. I'm assuming he found them when he left for school."

Lily popped another orange slice into her mouth. "What did the note say?"

"The first bite always tastes the best."

Lily gave Noelle a puzzled look. "What does that mean?"

"Remember when we were in Girl Scouts and we had to earn our cooking badges?"

"Don't remind me." Lily groaned. "It took me two days to clean up my mother's kitchen. I made such a mess. What made me think I could make a pineapple upside-down cake?"

"For my badge, I made a batch of chocolate chip cookies. And they were the *worst* cookies in the world. I think I forgot to add the sugar. When they came out of the oven, Charlie was dropping something off. I offered him a cookie, and he said when it came to chocolate chip cookies the first bite always tastes the best. Well, not *that* day! It was all he could do to swallow the first bite."

"Aha! A clue!"

"That's right!" Noelle exclaimed triumphantly. "Beach Girl might take credit for the cookies, but I'll expose her by reminding Charlie of what I wrote in the note and when he said it to me."

"Don't you mean *Celia*?" Lily teased, echoing Noelle's words from the day before.

Noelle stuck her tongue out.

"I almost forgot to tell you!" Lily exclaimed,

reaching into her shoulder bag. "My Secret Santa left me a gift." She pulled out a green ribbon. "What do you think?"

"Very pretty. It goes great with your red hair."

"I figured I'd wear it to the dance. Sort of as a clue to my Secret Santa."

"My Secret Santa left me a gift too," Noelle revealed.

"Really? What?"

"A Christmas angel. And I think it was left by Charlie!"

"Why do you think it was Charlie?" Lily asked.

Noelle explained her theory and Lily shook her head. "Don't you think that's wishful thinking?"

"Why do you always have to be such a downer?" Noelle huffed.

"I'm just trying to keep you grounded," Lily said.

"Burst my bubble is more like it!"

"There's still three more days leading up to the dance. Maybe I'm wrong. We'll just have to wait and see!"

★   ★   ★

Celia's first class after lunch was Art. The class was an elective so there was a mix of sophomores, juniors, and seniors. It was her favorite class not only because she loved painting and sketching, but also because Jake was in the class with her.

All morning she'd been running their conversation through her mind. She couldn't wait to see him again. Lunch had once again been Amber- and Shawna-free, because today there had been a meeting of the Fine Arts committee, which they were both members of. Could her day get any better?

When Celia got to class, she looked around for Jake but didn't see him anywhere. When the second bell rang, he still hadn't arrived, much to her disappointment. He hadn't cut the class, had he? Mr. Catini had just started discussing that day's project when an out-of-breath Jake arrived, along with Eva Digiorno.

"Sorry I'm late," he apologized. "I hit traffic on my way back to school."

"Me too." She giggled.

Celia knew that seniors were allowed to have lunch off campus. From Jake's windblown hair and clothes, it looked like he had been speeding back to school. With Eva probably on the back of his motorcycle.

Celia tried not to feel jealous. She knew Jake and Eva weren't dating. But Eva had gotten to spend time alone with Jake!

"Apology accepted, but you're both still late," Mr. Catini said, filling out two detention slips and handing one to Jake and one to Eva. "After school today."

That was so unfair! Celia thought. Jake had apologized. What more did Mr. Catini want?

Jake crumpled up the detention slip and put it in his back pocket on his way to his desk, which was right next to Celia's.

Mr. Catini went back to explaining that day's project, which was to sketch a still life. Looking around the classroom, Celia decided she was going to sketch a budding African violet on the windowsill.

"Know what you're going to sketch yet?" Celia asked.

Jake pointed to a soda bottle that was also on the windowsill.

Celia began sketching with her black pencil.

She kept looking up from her sketch pad and back to the plant. As the image formed, she started using her colored pencils. First green for the leaves, then purple for the flowering buds, then red for the pot the plant was in.

"How come you decided to sketch the violets?" Jake asked.

"Purple is my favorite color and I've always been drawn to things that are purple," Celia said, taking a peek at Jake's sketch. What she saw startled her. Jake *had* sketched a soda bottle, but it didn't look like any soda bottle she'd ever seen before! It looked like a soda bottle from another planet.

"Pretty cool, huh?" he said. "It's very surreal, don't you think?"

As Jake was showing Celia his sketch, Mr. Catini reached her desk. He took a look at Jake's sketch and sighed. "Mr. Morrisey, that is not the class assignment."

"But it looks good, doesn't it?" Jake said.

"That's beside the point. You were supposed to do a still life. That means sketching what you see."

Jake rolled his eyes. "That's boring. Doing the sketch my way keeps my interest."

"And it gets you an F unless you redo it."

"You can't give me an F," Jake complained. "I did the assignment."

"Incorrectly!"

Jake crumpled up his sketch and threw it on the floor. "Fine! I'll redo it!"

"Thank you."

"Why do you always fight with Mr. Catini?" Celia asked after he walked away.

Jake gave Celia a cocky smile. "I like to keep him on his toes, Ceel. Besides, it's the only bit of fun I get to have in this place."

Celia picked up Jake's crumpled sketch and smoothed it out. "You're a really talented artist, Jake. You should listen to his comments. Maybe you could become an artist one day."

"I don't want to be an artist."

"What do you want to be?"

Jake shrugged. "I don't know. All I do know is that I hate this class and I can't wait until June when it's over!"

June! Celia didn't even want to think about June. June meant Jake would be graduating and then she'd never see him again!

★   ★   ★

At the end of the day, Froggy was waiting for Jake outside of detention. He knew Jake was working later that day at Icing on the Cake, but he was too impatient to wait until then. Besides, he had a feeling Jake would wind up heading this way and he wasn't wrong.

"Don't you ever get tired of this room?" Froggy asked as he followed him inside.

"It's my home away from home," Jake said, plopping down in a chair and propping his boots up on a desk.

"You better take those off before Mrs. Bedford gets here."

"What's she going to do? Give me detention?"

"Yes!"

"Loosen up, Frogster!"

"Look, I can't stay very long. I've got to be somewhere else. Were you able to find out anything about Celia?"

Jake nodded. "A ton of stuff."

"Really?" Froggy's face lit up. "Like what?"

Jake handed him a slip of paper. "I wrote it all down. This should help you out."

Froggy couldn't help himself. He threw his arms around Jake and gave him a hug.

"Whoa!" Jake exclaimed, pulling back. "Watch it with the warm and fuzzy stuff!"

"Sorry!" Froggy apologized, racing out of the detention room. He was so excited! Thanks to Jake's list he was going to have a chance with Celia. The candy cane had been a no-brainer, but now he had what he needed. He'd be able to get Celia gifts that were really personal. Gifts that showed he cared.

He couldn't wait to show her how much he cared!

Chapter Nine

No matter how old she got, Celia would always love toy stores.

The first thing she noticed whenever she walked into one was the smell. She could never figure out what it was, but she loved it. It was very sweet, like a combination of baby powder and hot wax. Then there were the bright lights. The colorful packages. The shiny plastic. She could spend hours walking from one aisle to another, wanting to buy everything she saw.

That afternoon she was going toy shopping. Ryan Grant, who was in her Spanish II class, had told her he was heading up the school's Toys for Tots program and needed help buying toys. She'd immediately volunteered.

As she approached the toy store, she could see

some other familiar faces from school waiting outside, stomping their feet in the cold, puffs of air coming out of their mouths. It was a small group: Noelle Kramer and Lily Norris, Connor Hughes and Simon Larson. And Freddy.

"Everyone's here!" Ryan announced, catching sight of her. "Let's go shopping!"

"What's she doing here?" Lily hissed into Noelle's ear as they followed Ryan into the toy store.

"The same thing we are," Noelle answered, unwinding the teal scarf around her neck and pulling off the pompom hat she was wearing. "Buying toys for underprivileged kids."

Lily unbuttoned her red duffel coat, pushing the hood off her head. "I thought popular girls only cared about themselves."

"Be nice!" Noelle said. "Besides, it's good that she's here."

"It is?"

"Uh-huh. If we talk to her, maybe we can find out what she's got up her sleeve for Charlie."

Lily groaned. "Charlie, Charlie, Charlie! Why does everything always come back to Charlie?"

"Because it just does!" Noelle insisted as Ryan started clapping his hands to get everyone's attention.

"We've got a thousand dollars to spend thanks to the generosity of our classmates and teachers," he announced. "I think the best thing to do is grab some shopping carts and start filling them up. Remember, we're buying for all ages."

"Why don't we divide ourselves into groups?" Celia suggested. "Lily and Noelle and I can shop for the girls and you guys can shop for the boys."

"Great idea! Very organized," Ryan said. "I like the way you think, Celia."

"He likes the way she thinks," Lily hissed under her breath. "Is she going after both Grant brothers?"

"Shh!" Noelle whispered as she grabbed a shopping cart and headed in the direction of the doll aisle.

"What is it about guys and toys that make loud noises?" Celia asked Froggy as Simon and Connor aimed ray guns at each other, pulling the triggers so a loud zapping sound filled the toy store.

Froggy just shrugged as he and Celia walked down the game aisle.

Say something! he scolded himself. *Say something!*

But he didn't say anything. He just walked alongside her. Every so often, she would pick up a game like Scrabble or Monopoly or Sorry and put it into the shopping cart she was pushing. He wondered what it would be like playing a board game with her. Would she be playing for fun or was she one of those players who had to win?

But the one thing he was wondering about — the *big* thing he couldn't stop wondering about — was if Celia was romantically interested in Ryan. He'd never seen them together at school so he'd been surprised when she had joined them.

"How do you know Ryan?" Celia asked.

"We're in the same gym class," Froggy answered, finally finding his voice. "How about you?"

"Ryan's in my Spanish class. We sit next to each other."

Ryan probably talks to you every day. Unlike me, who never says anything.

"He told me he was coming shopping today and needed help," Celia continued. "I couldn't say no. I can't bear the idea of some underprivileged kid not finding a present under their tree on Christmas Day. It breaks my heart!"

Talk to her! Froggy screamed at himself. *Tell her you feel the same way! This is something you both have in common!*

But Froggy only nodded, his voice once again gone, beating himself up for blowing this golden opportunity to get to know Celia.

"Hey, Froggy!" Ryan called out. "We need your help figuring out which is the best Lego to buy."

"I better go catch up with Noelle and Lily," Celia said, turning her cart down an aisle.

You blew it! You blew it! You blew it! Froggy scolded himself as he watched Celia walk away. He sighed and then patted his shirt pocket. At least he still had the list that Jake had given him.

"Look!" Noelle exclaimed. "Silly Putty! I used to love playing with this when I was a kid." She threw a couple of Silly Putty eggs into her cart. "These are the perfect stocking stuffers."

Walking down the aisles was like a trip down memory lane for Noelle. Everywhere she looked, she saw toys that she had played with while growing up. Etch A Sketch. My Little Pony. Tickle Me Elmo. Barbie.

"Can you believe all this Barbie stuff?" Lily asked as they stopped their shopping carts in front of a huge Barbie display. "There are so many to choose from!"

"I still have my Barbie dolls," Celia confessed as she joined Noelle and Lily.

Noelle could see she looked nervous, but what was there to be nervous about? She and Lily didn't bite! She gave Celia a smile to put her at ease. "Me too."

"So do I," Lily said, "although most of mine are bald from when my brothers used to scalp them."

"Did you have ever have one of these?" Celia asked, picking up a Barbie styling head.

"Of course!" Noelle exclaimed. "I used to play beauty parlor with that." She looked around to make sure none of the guys were around. "Sometimes I'll still use it before trying a new hairstyle out on myself!"

"My little cousins don't like playing with

Barbie dolls," Lily said. "For them, the hot dolls are Bratz."

Celia made a face. "Ick! I don't like those at all. They look weird."

"But they're what's selling," Lily said. "We should buy some."

"Okay," Celia agreed, "but we'll have to throw in a few Barbies."

"Absolutely!" Lily exclaimed.

"Shopping for little kids is so much fun," Celia said as she checked the price on a baby doll.

"It's much easier than Secret Santa shopping," Noelle casually mentioned, waiting to see what Celia would say.

"Tell me about it," Celia sighed. "Guys are so hard to shop for."

"You have to buy a Secret Santa gift for a guy?" Noelle asked.

"Oops!" Celia covered her mouth with her hand. "I guess I let the cat out of the bag!"

"Today I left a gift for the guy whose name I picked," Lily said. "It was a complete disaster."

"Me too!" Celia exclaimed.

Noelle felt like doing the Snoopy happy dance. That was exactly what she wanted to hear!

Apparently Celia didn't have a clue about what Charlie liked and didn't like.

"Hopefully I'll get the next gift right," Celia said.

Hopefully you won't, Noelle thought.

Lily hated to admit it, but Celia wasn't as bad as she thought she was. True, she hung out with two Glamazons who were obsessed with shopping and guys, but she didn't seem that way at all. How had she become friends with them?

Lily left Noelle and Celia in the doll aisle. She told them she was going to get some boxes of crayons and magic markers, but what she was really going to do was pull a Nancy Drew and see if she could discover any info on Connor.

She was filling her arms with a pile of coloring books when she heard Simon and Connor talking in the next aisle. She leaned closer to a wall of books, trying to hear what they were saying on the other side. They were talking about cars, and Connor was making an argument as to why a Corvette was the only car to own. Hmmm. She couldn't afford to buy Connor a Corvette, but maybe she'd be able to get him the car of his dreams another way. She had to admit, it was a clever idea. And it wouldn't cost much!

She grabbed a couple of boxes of crayons and magic markers and then hurried back to Noelle and Celia.

"Think I'll pass my oral in Debate tomorrow?" Connor asked Simon after he finished his speech on Corvettes and added a model airplane kit to their shopping cart.

"You sound like you know your stuff," Simon said.

"Well, Mr. Ellingsworth loves his Corvette so I figured if I did my oral essay on one, I'd get a better grade. Personally, I can't stand them! I think they're one of the worst cars around. My uncle Mike used to have one and he was constantly taking it to his auto mechanic. Give me a Mercedes any day!"

Celia found herself liking Noelle and Lily. They were so much fun to talk to. Why hadn't she met them when she first moved to town instead of Amber and Shawna?

She wanted to invite them to come over to her house during the Christmas break, but she couldn't. Amber had already planned out a week's worth of activities for her and Shawna. One day they would be going ice-skating at Rockefeller Center. The next they would be going to see a matinee on Broadway. Another day they would be going skiing, and then they would be hitting all the after-Christmas sales.

She wished she could invite Noelle and Lily to come along, but she didn't know what Amber and Shawna's reaction would be. She didn't think they'd be too happy about it, but why did she care? Noelle and Lily were nice. She liked them. She wanted to be friends with them. What was so wrong with mixing together groups of friends? Why couldn't she be friends with whoever she wanted? Amber and Shawna as well as Noelle and Lily.

Why did she have to choose?

And if she did have to choose, would she wind up making the right choice?

★   ★   ★

"I can't believe how generous the store manager was!" Noelle exclaimed thirty minutes later as they all left the toy store.

"Everyone has a little bit of Santa Claus in them," Ryan said.

Noelle playfully squeezed Ryan's nose, which was turning red from the cold winter air. "I thought you didn't believe in Santa!"

"Guess I was wrong."

"Guess you were," Noelle said smugly.

When the manager of the toy store found out Ryan was buying toys for the Toys for Tots program, he instantly donated an extra shopping cart of toys. All the toys would be delivered to Ryan's house the next day, where they would be wrapped and then dropped off at the local post office.

"Get ready to start wrapping!" Ryan announced to everyone. "My house. Tomorrow. After school. Be there!"

"I don't know about the rest of you," Froggy said, "but I'm hungry. Why don't we all head to Icing on the Cake, where I work. Everyone can use my employee discount!"

"I never say no to cupcakes!" Ryan exclaimed. "Sounds like a plan."

"A very sweet plan," Celia added, giving Froggy a smile. "That's so nice of you."

Once again, Froggy was speechless. But at least he managed to smile back at Celia.

Shawna's feet were killing her. If she had known she and Amber were going to go Christmas shopping after school, she never would have worn her high-heeled boots today. Even though they made her legs look great, they weren't made for walking for hours. But she hadn't known. After the bell for last class rang, Amber told her they were going to the mall.

She and Amber had spent the entire afternoon going from store to store. Shawna had been able to cross a few names off her Christmas list, but everything Amber had bought had been for herself. Now they were loaded down with so many shopping bags, they could barely carry them.

"Simon was supposed to meet us here!" Amber raged, staring at her watch. "And I told him to bring Connor. I can't believe they stood us up!"

"Maybe something came up?"

Amber gave Shawna an icy stare. "More important than us?"

Shawna shrugged as she sat down on a bench. Aaaah! It felt good to be off her feet.

"And where did Celia disappear to?" Amber asked. "I couldn't find her after last class."

"You two look like you've been hitting the stores!"

Shawna turned around to see Mindy Yee headed their way. She was wearing a sage-dyed shearling jacket with dyed fox trim. Shawna had seen the jacket in the latest issue of *Vogue* and knew it cost at least three thousand dollars.

"*Love* the coat," Amber squealed, running her hand down a sleeve. "Is it new?"

Mindy turned up the collar and whirled around. "An early Christmas from my parents."

Mindy's parents owned a chain of upscale Chinese restaurants called House of Yee. Money was no object for them. Whatever Mindy saw in the pages of a fashion magazine, she usually got to buy. The jacket was probably only one of the many fabulous Christmas presents she would receive that year.

"It's yummy!" Amber raved.

"Buy anything fab?" Mindy asked, peeking into their shopping bags. Shawna had to resist the urge to slap away her poking hands. Mindy was such a snoop! "But I don't see the boy-friends," she said, looking around. "You haven't dumped them, have you? Because if you did that would mean you'd be dateless for Friday night's dance."

Amber gave a nasty laugh, looking at Mindy like she was crazy. "Do you *really* think we'd be without dates on Friday night?"

Mindy shrugged, examining her French manicure. "I don't know." She held a hand out to Shawna. "You like? I just got them done." Then she turned back to Amber. "Tell me."

Actually, now that Mindy mentioned it, Shawna realized that Connor *hadn't* asked her if she wanted to go to the Christmas dance. Which meant she *was* dateless. She found herself starting to get angry. What was he waiting for? He did want to take her, didn't he?

"We still have boyfriends," Amber said, giving Mindy her *don't mess with me* look.

Mindy ignored it. "Really?" Her head swirled from the left to the right and then back again, her glossy black hair swinging back and forth. "Have Simon and Connor gone invisible? Because I don't see them."

"They're not always with us," Amber said.

"They used to be," Mindy smirked. "Besides, I thought I heard you tell Simon at lunch that you were going Christmas shopping and you wanted him to meet you."

Amber gave Mindy a steely glare. "You must have heard wrong."

Mindy shook her head. "I don't think so."

Shawna decided it was time to change the subject before Mindy pushed Amber too far. "Has your Secret Santa left you anything yet, Mindy?"

Mindy rolled her eyes. "Yes. A gift certificate for a Big Gulp at 7-Eleven. *Sooo* classy."

A Big Gulp for a big mouth, Shawna thought. *Seems like the perfect gift to me.*

"I better get going," Mindy said. "I still need to find a dress for the dance! If I don't find anything here, I may have to go into Manhattan." She waved her fingers. "Bye!"

"I can't stand her!" Amber spat out after Mindy left. "She always has to know everyone's business. If her parents weren't so rich and she didn't throw such expensive parties, I wouldn't have anything to do with her."

Which is the same reason why Mindy is friends with you, Shawna thought.

"We need someone to help us carry these bags," Amber said, her eyes scanning the mall. Then she saw a short skinny guy with a head of orange-red hair heading out of Barnes & Noble. She jabbed Shawna in the side. "Doesn't that nerd go to school with us?"

Shawna followed Amber's pointing finger. The guy did look familiar. "I think so. But I'm not sure."

"Hey!" Amber called out. "Hey, you!" She snapped her fingers. "Over here!"

The nerd finally looked up from the magazine he was reading and gazed in their direction. Amber nodded her head and he came racing over.

"You go to North Ridge High, don't you?" she said.

"I do," he said. "I'm David Benson."

"Then you know who we are." Amber handed him a bunch of shopping bags. "We need help carrying these. You don't mind helping us, do you?"

"Of course not!"

Amber added a row of shopping bags to each of David's arms. Then she piled a stack of boxes in his outstretched arms. "Make sure you don't drop anything!" she ordered. Then she turned to Shawna. "I need something hot to drink. Starbucks is too far away so let's go to Icing on the Cake."

"My best friend works there," David said. "I can probably get you a discount."

Amber rolled her eyes. "Is that supposed to impress me?" she whispered to Shawna.

"Look what I got from my Secret Santa today," Shawna said, reaching into her coat pocket and holding out a reindeer pin. "It was waiting at my locker after last class. I think it's supposed to be Rudolph's girlfriend. See, she has a pink bow on the top of her head."

Amber gave Shawna a horrified look. "You're not going to wear it, are you?"

"Why not?"

"It's so cheap-looking!"

David caught up with them and peeked from behind the stack of boxes in his arms. "I think it's pretty cute. My Secret Santa left me a DVD of the last X-Men movie. Did you know it has ten deleted scenes added? I already own it, but I can probably swap it with someone."

"Did we ask for your opinion?" Amber demanded. "This is a private conversation between me and my friend."

"Sorry," David mumbled.

"Your job is to carry and not talk. Got it?"

"Got it."

Shawna slipped the pin back into her pocket. "So what are we going to do about Friday night?"

"What do you mean?"

"If we don't have dates. We can't show up alone."

"You don't have dates?" David exclaimed, a note of disbelief in his voice.

Amber whirled around. "What did I say about talking?" she demanded.

"Sorry," David apologized. "But if you need dates for Friday night, my best friend and I would love to take both of you."

"Is he crazy?" Amber whispered to Shawna.

"I think he's serious," Shawna whispered back. She could just imagine the look of glee on Mindy Yee's face if she and Amber showed up at the dance with two nerds. She'd be text-messaging so fast, her thumbs would fall off!

"How about it?" David asked excitedly.

Amber didn't even bother answering.

★　　★　　★

Once they arrived at Icing on the Cake, Froggy was so busy getting drinks and cupcakes for everyone he hardly had a chance to talk with Celia. That wasn't a bad thing, because he could see she was hanging out with Jake. The more she hung out with Jake, the more Jake would be able to find out about her and then he'd be able to report back!

When Celia walked into Icing on the Cake, she was surprised to see Jake standing behind the cash register. She had no idea he worked at the coffeehouse. She didn't come to Icing on the Cake very often because Amber and Shawna always preferred going to Starbucks when they needed a caffeine fix. She was going to have to start coming here more often!

She slid into an armchair that was close to the cash register and gave Jake a wave.

"Hey! Ceel! What's up?" he said, coming over with an order pad. "What can I get you?"

"Peppermint tea would be nice."

He scribbled it down on his pad.

"How was detention?" she asked.

"Same as it was yesterday and the day before and the day before that."

"You should try being good," she said.

Jake shook his head. "Nah. Being good is boring. Wanna know why?"

"Why?"

He leaned down, close to Celia's ear. As he did, the scent of his cologne filled her nose, along with the scent of the black leather vest he was wearing. "Being bad is better," he whispered. "You should try it."

Celia swallowed over the lump in her throat. "I don't know anything about being bad."

"Maybe I'll have to show you," Jake said as he left to get her tea.

"Maybe you will," Celia said to herself, her heart suddenly pounding with excitement. "Maybe you will."

"One hot chocolate with extra marshmallows," Ryan said, handing the cup to Noelle.

Noelle looked at the cup in amazement. "How did you known I like extra marshmallows?"

Ryan rolled his eyes. "We've been living next

door to each other since the third grade, Noelle. Give me a little credit. There's a lot I know about you."

"Like what?" she challenged, blowing on her hot chocolate to cool it off.

"Yellow is your favorite color, spring is your favorite season, you like ketchup on your hot dogs, not mustard, you love romantic comedies, your favorite TV show is *Grey's Anatomy*, and not only do you believe in Santa Claus, you also believe in Prince Charming."

"I do not!"

"Don't deny it! You're always first in line whenever a new Disney cartoon comes out, you own all the Disney classics, like *Cinderella*, *Snow White*, *Sleeping Beauty*, and *The Little Mermaid*, and you *devour* romance novels."

"Okay, you've proven your point," Noelle grumbled, taking a tiny sip of her hot chocolate so she wouldn't burn her tongue. "You know a lot about me. But I know just as much about you."

"Prove it."

"Hockey is your favorite sport, *Jackass* is your favorite movie, the only vegetable you'll eat is celery, your favorite color is blue, you love horror movies — although I don't know why, they're so horrible to watch — and you're very generous when it comes to helping others who aren't as fortunate as we are." Noelle popped an unmelted marshmallow into her mouth. "How'd I do?"

"Pretty good, but you still don't know everything about me."

"Like what?"

Ryan shook his head. "I'm not telling. You're going to have to figure it out yourself."

Noelle took another sip of her hot chocolate and noticed Ryan staring at her, his lips twitching. "Why are you looking at me so funny?"

"You've got a hot-chocolate mustache," Ryan said, rubbing a finger under his nose.

How embarrassing! Noelle looked around for a napkin, but Ryan came to her rescue.

"Here, let me," he said, gently wiping the mustache away.

"How long did I have that on my face?"

"Awhile."

"Why didn't you say something sooner?"

"You looked so cute."

Noelle scowled at Ryan as she took another sip of her hot chocolate, making sure she didn't get any foam on her upper lip. Charlie would have told her instantly that she had a foam mustache, but not Ryan. He had to laugh at her, the way he used to when they were eight years old. Oooh, he made her so mad!

"Where's your sense of humor, Noelle?" he asked with a smile.

"The Grinch stole it."

"We'll have to get him to bring it back."

Noelle stuck her tongue out at Ryan. "Bah, humbug!"

Chapter Ten

Lily was totally confused. She had bought herself a brownie with walnuts and then joined Connor and Simon at the table where they were sitting. She had offered both of them a piece of her brownie, but Connor had passed.

"Are you sure you don't want some?" she asked him a second time.

Connor shook his head. "I hate nuts."

"You hate nuts?"

If he hated nuts, why had he checked out a copy of *Nutty Desserts* from the school library? And so much for her idea of buying him a stocking full of peanuts as a Secret Santa gift!

"I'll have his piece," Simon said, reaching for another chunk of the brownie.

"I'm going to see what other desserts they have," Connor said, leaving the table.

What was she supposed to do now? She couldn't go running after him! Hopefully he'd come back.

"This is really good," Simon said, inhaling Connor's piece of the brownie.

Why did guys always eat so fast? Lily wondered. It was like they were afraid someone was going to take their food away!

Staring at Simon, a thought popped into Lily's head. Why hadn't she thought of it sooner? Simon and Connor were best friends. Simon probably knew more about Connor than anyone else.

"Doing anything special during the Christmas break?" she asked.

"We're flying out to California to see my grandparents. How about you?"

"I'm going to be a couch potato. Rent lots of DVDs."

"What kind?"

She knew Connor liked horror movies. Maybe she could start a conversation about them and find something out.

"I love horror movies so I thought I'd rent a bunch of those. I still haven't seen *Saw III* or *The Grudge 2*. I thought I might also rent some old stuff. You know, *Halloween*, *Scream*, *Friday the 13th*, *Nightmare on Elm Street*."

"Have you seen *Freddy vs. Jason*? It's wicked-intense!"

Was that some sort of new guy adjective? From the way Simon was grinning, wicked-intense must be a good thing.

Lily tried to remember the titles of a bunch of recent horror movies. Personally, she hated them. Whenever she went to see one in a movie theater, she sat with her eyes squinted shut, peeking from behind her hands. She hated when the killer would pop out unexpectedly. She much preferred renting them. That way she could fast-forward through the creepy parts.

Simon started telling her about horror movies she should rent. Each one sounded more gruesome than the next. How did guys watch them? But she pretended to be interested, hoping that an idea for another Secret Santa gift would pop into her head. She already had the idea she came up with at the toy store. She just needed to come up with two more Secret Santa gifts by Friday.

Simon couldn't believe how much fun he was having talking to Lily. It was very rare to find a girl who liked horror movies. And it was nice of her to share her brownie with him. Walnut fudge brownies were his favorite, but he loved any kind of dessert with nuts.

Why had he never noticed her before? She wasn't as glamorous as Amber, but she was pretty in her own way. She could be a knockout if she wanted — but he got the sense that wasn't her personal style.

"The revival house across town is having a horror festival next month," he said. "You should check it out. I'm definitely going to."

He hoped she picked up on the clue he'd dropped. After all, he couldn't ask her out on a date. He was still dating Amber and he wasn't the kind of guy who cheated. But who knew what might happen in the new year? He had the feeling he might be single again.

Dating Amber was becoming a drag. Yeah, she was one of the hottest girls at North Ridge

High, but after two months of dating her, he'd come to realize that she was obsessed with herself and who she hung out with. Everything and everybody had to be A-list with her. Who cared as long as you were having a good time? Amber's style was *not* his style. But as much as he wanted to break up with her, he couldn't do it right before Christmas. That would be really low.

Lily was the complete opposite of Amber. Amber never would have given up an afternoon for the Toys for Tots program.

He remembered the way Lily was at the toy store as they were picking out toys. It was like she was glowing with happiness at the thought of helping the underprivileged kids they were shopping for. Noelle and Celia had been the same way.

After breaking up with Amber, he didn't know how soon he'd want to start dating again, but with a girl like Lily around, who knew?

"You are *not* going to believe this!" Amber screeched, coming to a halt in front of Icing on the Cake. She pointed at the plateglass window and Shawna pressed her face against it. Inside the coffeehouse, she saw Celia. And Simon. And Connor!

Amber flung open the front door and stormed into Icing on the Cake. Shawna hurried behind her, knowing a human volcano was about to explode.

"Do you know how long we waited at the mall for you and Connor?" she yelled at Simon. "You were supposed to help us with our Christmas shopping! When you never showed up, I started worrying." Tears filled her eyes. "I thought something bad might have happened to you! Like a car accident!"

Shawna had to give Amber credit. She was *quite* the actress. And she was making sure to pile on the guilt before going in for the kill.

She wiped away her tears. "But no! There was no accident! You were here having a good time while we were worried sick!"

"Is it okay if I put these down?" David gasped, out of breath. He didn't wait for an answer. Instead, he collapsed onto a couch, dropping the packages onto a cushion.

"I can see how worried you were," Simon said dryly. "I guess you must have shopped through it."

Amber ignored the comment, turning her attention to Celia. "And you!" she lashed out. "Where have you been?"

"I was helping with the Toys for Tots program. We all were."

"Who's *we*?"

"Me, Simon, Connor, Ryan, Lily, Noelle, and Freddy."

"Was this some sort of extra credit assignment I didn't know about?" Amber nastily asked.

"No," Froggy said, his voice cracking. "We were all doing something in the spirit of the season. You might want to try it yourself someday."

Amber glared at Froggy. "I wasn't talking to you, Toad!"

"We were just finishing up here," Celia said, slipping into her coat. "Why don't we leave together?" she suggested, hustling Amber and Shawna out of Icing on the Cake, with Simon and Connor right behind her.

Froggy didn't know where he had found the courage to talk back to Amber. The words came out of his mouth before he could stop them, but he'd been so angry. He couldn't believe how horrible she was and he couldn't stand to see the way she was talking to Celia. But even more shocking was the fact that David was with them.

"What are you doing with Amber and Shawna?" he asked, racing over to David's side.

"What does it look like I'm doing?" David asked as he got off the couch, loading himself back up with packages, his voice filled with excitement. "I'm getting 'in' with them!"

Froggy put a hand on David's forehead. "Are you feeling feverish? There's no way we'd ever be in with the two of them."

"They don't have dates for Friday night's dance," he whispered, eyes wide with glee.

"So?"

"So? So? Is that all you can say?" David grabbed Froggy by the front of his shirt and shook him. "Don't you see? We can take them!"

"Okay, you definitely need to see a doctor because you're making *no* sense. Girls like Amber and Shawna do *not* go out with guys like us. They go out with guys like Simon and Connor. Or guys like Jake!"

"Jake?" David snorted in disbelief. "What does he have that we don't have?"

"Besides great hair, rock-hard muscles, a

motorcycle, and lots of attitude? His pick of any girl in the place." Froggy jerked a thumb over one shoulder. "As you can see for yourself."

David glanced at the line of girls waiting by the cash register, all of them gazing dreamily at Jake. "Oh."

Before Froggy could say anything else, Amber stuck her head back inside. "Donald! Are you going to sit on that couch all night? I want to go home and I want to go home with my packages *now*."

"She doesn't even know your name!" Froggy exclaimed.

"It was noisy at the mall," David said. "She couldn't hear me."

Froggy sighed.

"Gotta go!" David said, staggering under his load of packages before finding his balance. "I'll let you know what happens. Bye!"

"Did you buy yourself a dress for the dance on Friday night?" Connor asked as they waited for David outside Icing on the Cake.

The words slipped out of Shawna's mouth before she could stop them. "Why do you care?"

Connor gave her a confused look. "Aren't we going together?"

Shawna shrugged. "I don't know. Are we?"

"Hey, what's with the attitude?"

Shawna could hear a pissed-off tone creeping into Connor's voice. Which made her mad. If anyone deserved to be pissed off, it was her! "No attitude."

"So are we going to the dance on Friday night?"

"I don't know!" Shawna snapped, losing her temper the way Amber had a few minutes earlier. "You never bothered to ask me!"

"I just assumed we were going together."

"Well you assumed wrong!" Shawna shouted before she could stop herself. Of course she wanted to go to the dance with Connor, but she wanted to be asked. She didn't want to be taken for granted! How was she supposed to know he wanted to take her to the dance? He hadn't taken her out in weeks!

"Are you saying you don't want to go with me? Are you going with someone else?"

"You'll just have to wait until Friday night to find out."

Connor shook his head. "I don't have time for

these games," he said, walking away. "I've got to get to work."

"Me too," Simon said, breaking off his own conversation with Amber and hurrying after Connor. "I'll drop you off."

"Great!" Amber exclaimed. "There goes our ride home!"

"Speaking of home, I better get going or I'm going to be late for dinner," Celia said, starting to head off after Simon and Connor.

"Not so fast," Amber said, sinking her nails into Celia's arm. "We need to have a little talk."

"About what?"

Shawna could see that Celia looked uncomfortable. She wondered why.

Amber tilted her head in the direction of the bakery. "That thug you were talking to."

"Who?"

"Jake Morrisey. I also saw you talking with him at school this morning."

"He was asking me when an assignment was due. We're in the same Art class."

"That's why you were talking to him for so long?"

"Were you timing us? We started talking about other things."

"Like what?"

"Are you my mother?" Celia asked, annoyed, shaking her arm free of Amber's grip.

Shawna couldn't believe Celia was talking back to Amber!

"Girls like us don't talk to guys like Jake Morrisey," Amber said.

"Why not? He's a nice guy. What's the problem?"

Oooh! This was getting good! What was Celia going to do next? Shawna wondered.

"Because we don't!" Amber snapped, eyes blazing. "We're A-list and Jake Morrisey isn't even *on* a list."

"I didn't know," Celia said softly.

Shawna was bummed. She had thought Celia might keep standing up to Amber, but like everyone else, she had backed down.

"Now you do."

"I've got to get home," Celia said. "I'll see you both at school tomorrow."

"How stupid could she be?" Amber muttered as Celia disappeared down the street.

"She made a mistake. Cut her some slack."

"If guys like Jake Morrisey start talking to her,

then they're going to start talking to *us*. Do you really want that?"

"Jake *is* a hottie," Shawna giggled.

"I don't believe you!"

"Well he is!"

"Where is that nerd?" Amber huffed just as David came out with their packages. "It's about time!"

"Sorry," David apologized. "The boxes kept falling out of my arms."

"You didn't break anything, did you?" Amber asked. "Because if you did, you're paying for it!"

"Nothing broke," David promised.

To make David's load easier, Shawna took two boxes off the top of his wobbly pile as they followed Amber down the street.

The first stop was Amber's house. After dropping her off with her packages, David walked with Shawna three houses down.

"This is where I live," she said as they approached a house covered with twinkling white lights. On the front lawn there was a lighted Mr. and Mrs. Snowman with a MERRY CHRISTMAS sign between them. After David walked her to her front door, she took her shopping bags from him. "Thanks for your help."

"Anytime." David stood in front of her, like he was waiting for something. He wasn't expecting a tip, was he? Then a horrifying thought popped into Shawna's mind. He didn't expect a *kiss*, did he?

At that moment, the front porch light came on and Shawna's mother stuck her head out.

"Shawna! It's about time! Dinner's ready." She glanced at David. "Who's this?"

"Someone from school."

"It looks like he was helping you carry your packages." She held out a hand. "I'm Darla Westin, Shawna's mother. Why don't you stay and have dinner with us?"

What was her mother doing? She didn't want David to stay for dinner. She shot him a look that said: *You will turn down my mother's invitation.*

"Thanks! I'd love to!" David exclaimed, his face lighting up. "Carrying those bags gave me an appetite."

"Wonderful!"

Shawna waited until her mother headed back inside. Then she grabbed David by the arm and pulled him to one side.

"Not so fast, buster," she warned. "If you breathe one word of this dinner to anyone, you are a dead man!"

"Who would I tell?" David innocently asked.

"Don't play dumb with me. I'm not going to be discussed in the boys' locker room, got it? I will hunt you down and kill you if I find out you've told *anyone* about tonight. Got it?"

David pressed his lips together and pretended he was turning a key. "My lips are sealed!"

Shawna released David's arm and walked inside, dropping her shopping bags at the foot of the staircase that led to the second floor. Then she sat on the last step and unzipped her boots, slipping her feet into a pair of fuzzy, blue bunny-rabbit slippers. She wiggled her toes. Sweet relief! Her feet felt *so* much better!

"Follow me," she said as she headed into the kitchen.

Her mother was at the stove, filling a bowl with mashed potatoes. The smell of roast chicken was thick in the air. Already sitting at the table were Shawna's two younger sisters. Chloe was a freshman at North Ridge High while Cassidy was in fifth grade. Shawna's father was sitting at the head of the table, his face buried in the financial section of the newspaper. Shawna gave him a kiss on the cheek before taking her seat at the country-style wooden table.

"This is David," she introduced. "You can sit over here," she said, pointing to the chair next to her.

"Is he your new boyfriend?" Cassidy asked, staring at David.

Shawna choked on the glass of water she was sipping. "N-n-no," she coughed as David started pounding on her back.

"Scary thought, huh?" David joked.

"Connor is still my boyfriend," Shawna said once she caught her breath.

But was he really? They'd had two fights today. He wasn't acting like he was her boyfriend. It hadn't helped that she had been so awful to him during their last fight. But her feelings were hurt!

"Really? Then how come we never see him anymore?" Chloe asked, peering at Shawna over the tops of her wire-rimmed glasses. "I can't remember the last time he came over."

"He's been busy," Shawna snapped in her *I don't want to talk about it* tone. Chloe hadn't started dating yet so she was clueless when it came to guys. Although maybe if she glammed herself up a bit, the guys would start calling. Cassidy was supercute, but Chloe downplayed her looks. Most days she looked like the BEFORE girl in makeover ads. Shawna wished Chloe would replace those granny glasses with contacts, do something with her hair instead of always pulling it back into a messy ponytail, and start sneaking into her closet to borrow her clothes!

"You look like the guy from *Mad* magazine," Cassidy told David.

"Alfred E. Neuman," David said. "Yeah, I know."

"He does not!" Chloe exclaimed. "I think you look more like Ron Howard, the film director, when he had hair. That's when he used to be an actor. Have you ever watched him on *Happy Days*, that sitcom set in the fifties? TV Land shows it all the time."

"Chloe lives for old TV shows," Shawna said, taking a biscuit from a basket and passing the basket to David. "She's always watching TV Land and Nick at Nite."

"Me too!" David exclaimed. "Which shows are your favorites?"

Dinner with David wasn't as bad as Shawna

had expected. He didn't focus all his attention on her, which was what she had been expecting him to do. The last thing she needed in her life was a lovesick nerd. He talked with both her sisters, as well as her parents. When dinner was over, he offered to help her mother clean up, but she shooed him out of the kitchen.

"What do you want to do now?" David asked.

Okay, it was time to put an end to things. She didn't want David thinking he could hang around for the rest of the night.

"*I'm* going to do my homework and *you're* going home," she announced, handing David his parka and marching him to the front door.

"Dinner was fun. We'll have to do it again. Maybe at my house next time."

Shawna didn't reply to his comment.

"Here's my cell phone number," he said, handing Shawna a piece of paper before she closed the front door in his face. "If you wind up needing a date for the dance, call me!"

Froggy was between customers when the phone rang at Icing on the Cake. When he picked it up, he was surprised to hear Celia's voice on the other end of the line.

"Hey, Celia. What's up?"

"Sorry I ran out so fast this afternoon. Things were getting kind of scary with Amber."

"Remember that scene from *The Wizard of Oz* when the Wicked Witch of the West first shows up? We witnessed it today."

Celia laughed. "You are bad!"

"What? It's the truth!"

Froggy couldn't believe it. He was talking with Celia! Maybe it was because she wasn't standing across from him, but the words were just flowing. And he was making her laugh!

"Thanks for sticking up for me, but you really didn't have to do that. I'm a big girl. I know how to take care of myself."

Froggy didn't think so. He had watched the scene through the front window when Amber had grabbed Celia by the arm. At first it looked like Celia was sticking up for herself, but then she had backed down. He wondered what they had been arguing about.

"Why are you friends with her? She's so mean."

"Amber's not so bad. You just have to get to know her."

"Thanks but no thanks."

Celia's next question caught Froggy off guard. "Is Jake around?"

Jake? Why did she want to talk with Jake?

"He's gone for the day. Want to leave a message?"

"That's okay. I just wanted to apologize for disappearing. I'll tell him tomorrow. Bye."

Froggy gave a sigh of relief as he hung up the phone. Phew! For a second there, he thought Celia was interested in Jake.

Chapter Eleven

The following morning another package was waiting on Noelle's front porch.

She had opened her front door slowly, hoping that when she looked down at the welcome mat, there would be another wrapped present.

And there was!

This package was wrapped in gold foil and had a purple bow on top. Like last time, there was a sealed note. Noelle decided to read the note first and ripped open the envelope. She gasped when she read what was written: *These kisses are sweet, but my kiss will be sweeter. Hope you'll want to try one!*

Noelle tore away the wrapping paper and found a box filled with dark chocolate kisses. She peeled the purple foil away from one and popped it into her mouth, savoring its taste and wondering which kiss her Secret Santa was referring to in the note. The ones she could eat or the one he was hoping to give her?

Noelle's heart instantly started pounding. The kisses *had* to be from Charlie. He knew she only loved dark chocolate kisses. She had told him on Halloween when he stopped by her house to drop off a package from his mother and inspected the candy in her candy bowl. In addition to the dark chocolate kisses in the bowl, there had been mini–Mounds bars and mini–Midnight Milky Ways.

"No Reese's Peanut Butter Cups?" he had asked with a sad face. "Or Almond Joys?"

"I buy our Halloween candy, and I only like dark chocolate, not milk chocolate," she had told him. "If any candy is left over after the trick-or-treaters come, I want to be able to eat it!"

Noelle ran her fingers over her lips. Would she be able to handle a kiss from Charlie? The thought of kissing him gave her goose bumps, especially when she remembered the nickname some of the girls at school had given him: Hot Lips!

Still in her pj's, she dashed back inside, tossed on her overcoat, and grabbed her latest present for Charlie from under the Christmas tree. The amount of wrapped packages underneath was slim, but hopefully there would be tons of presents by Christmas morning. And with her name on most of them!

She could feel the morning dew seeping into the bottom of her slippers as she raced across her front lawn to Charlie's house. Ick!

When she reached Charlie's front door, she left her second package for him and then hurried back home. She hoped he liked this second gift. She knew how much Charlie loved the beach — during the summer he worked at Jones Beach as a lifeguard. She had filled a box with colorful seashells of all different shapes and sizes that she had collected over the years and included a note. The note said: *Like these seashells, you're one of a kind!*

When she got back home, Noelle jumped into a steamy-hot shower. Then, wrapped in a fluffy towel, her hair in a turban, she stood in front of her closet, trying to decide what she wanted to wear.

Usually she dressed for warmth when the weather got colder, wearing oversized sweaters and turtlenecks, corduroy jeans, and fleece-lined boots. But she wanted to wear something chic and stylish today. An outfit that a guy would *notice*. If Charlie *was* her Secret Santa, she wanted him to see that she could look just as good as the seniors he was dating!

After rummaging through her closet, she decided to wear a sleeveless V-cut silk top in aquamarine and a black suede miniskirt matched with a silver chain belt. She put her hair in a French braid and for jewelry added a pair of silver hoop earrings — *very* Beyoncé from her *Ring the Alarm* video — and an arm of silver bangle bracelets. The fleece-lined boots were left in a corner. Instead, she slipped into a pair of high-heeled black leather boots that came just above the knee (again, very *Ring the Alarm*!).

She studied herself in the full-length mirror hanging on her closed bedroom door, pleased with what she saw.

Perfect.

She had achieved the look she wanted.

Older.

Sophisticated.

Now all she had to do was hope that Charlie noticed.

Celia hoped Jake would notice her.

She had dressed up for school today, deciding to go a little . . . hotter.

She was wearing an off-the-shoulder, pink, wrap chiffon top that tied with a funky jeweled brooch, a pair of slim-cut pink jeans, and studded platform boots. Instead of her hair being long and straight the way it usually was, she'd set it with rollers last night. When she'd taken them out this morning, she had supermodel hair — big and bouncy with lots of waves!

Her look was very Sandy at the end of *Grease*, just not all in black!

Guys always turned their heads when she walked down the hallways, but today they were doing it more than usual. Hmmm. Maybe she had overdone it. If *they* were noticing her, then Amber was *definitely* going to notice her.

And that wouldn't be a good thing.

She could already sense that Amber was suspicious, but Amber didn't know what to be suspicious of.

But given enough time, she would figure out that Celia was interested in Jake.

She needed to come up with a story by lunchtime — luckily she wasn't going to see Amber today until then — because once Amber saw her she was going to ask why she looked the way she did.

When she walked into Anatomy and Physiology, Freddy's eyes practically bugged out of his head.

"Wow!" he exclaimed, nearly jumping out of his seat. "You're all dressed up. What's the occasion?"

Okay, it was official.

If Freddy — who barely ever said more than two words to her — had noticed the way she was dressed, then she had overdone it.

However, on the positive side, if *Freddy* had noticed, then Jake definitely would!

"No special occasion. I found this outfit at the back of my closet and decided to wear it." She wondered if Amber would buy that story. Freddy seemed to.

"You look great. Really great."

Celia smiled at the compliment. Then her

smile grew wider as she approached her seat and saw what was sitting on top of it.

It was a small purple shopping bag.

Another gift from her Secret Santa!

Celia tossed her books to the floor and rummaged through the purple tissue paper inside the bag. She pulled out a purple pen, a purple pencil, a pack of grape gum, and a stuffed purple cow.

"What's with all the purple?" Freddy asked. "Is it your favorite color?"

"Yes, it is," she gasped as his question sank in.

Only one person at North Ridge High knew that purple was her favorite color.

Jake.

She had told him yesterday during Art class.

He had to be the one who left her this package.

Which meant he had to be her Secret Santa!

Froggy couldn't take his eyes off Celia. He'd never seen her look so gorgeous!

All he wanted to do was sit and stare at her, but he knew he'd freak her out if he did.

It was something only a nerd would do.

He needed a distraction.

He reached into his backpack, pulled out the copy of *Pride and Prejudice* that he had checked out of the library yesterday afternoon, and started reading where he last left off. Seconds later, he was aware of Celia standing next to him, holding out the pack of grape gum he had bought her.

"Want a piece?"

"Thanks," he said, taking a stick. "So you like all the stuff your Secret Santa bought for you?"

"I love it!"

Froggy was thrilled with her answer. He really wanted to outdo yesterday's gift.

"Are you reading that for English class?" she asked, pointing to his book.

He shook his head. "I'm reading it on my own."

"How come?" She blew a purple bubble and popped it, sucking the gum back into her mouth. "Most guys don't like Jane Austen."

"My mom rented the movie last weekend and made us all watch it. She likes to expose my father and me to culture. I wanted to see how close the movie was to the book. Sometimes they're different, you know? Plus, I figured it would impress my mom."

And you! Froggy thought.

Actually, he had rented the movie last night and only been able to watch half of it before falling asleep. All those English accents and weird costumes had bored him. And he couldn't believe that back then it was scandalous for a woman to show her ankle!

"I love Jane Austen," Celia said. "All the movies based on her books are great. *Sense and Sensibility* is my favorite. I love Kate Winslet in it. Hey, did you know that the movie *Clueless* is based on Jane Austen's novel *Emma?*"

"Really?" *Clueless* was a pretty funny movie. Maybe Hollywood should set all her novels in the present, rather than the past.

"Uh-huh."

Celia was a walking encyclopedia of Jane Austen information and began telling Froggy tons of facts.

He propped his chin in his hand and intently listened to every last word.

It meant he could stare at Celia to his heart's content!

★　　★　　★

When Celia got to Art class, she decided she wasn't going to say anything to Jake about her Secret Santa gift. She was going to wait and see if he said anything to her. After all, if he was her Secret Santa he was going to want to know if she found his gift and liked it, right?

Speaking of Secret Santa gifts . . .

Celia reached into her shoulder bag and pulled out a wrapped package. Making sure she wasn't seen, she slipped it on top of Jake's desk and then started flipping through her sketch pad for a clean page.

The classroom started filling up, and right before the final bell rang, Jake raced in.

"Right under the wire, Mr. Morrisey," Mr. Catini said, closing the classroom door as the bell rang.

Jake gave Celia a nod as he slipped into his seat. He glanced at the wrapped package on his desk and then shoved it to one side.

"Aren't you going to open your gift?" Celia asked, pointing at it.

Jake tossed it to Celia. "You do the honors, Ceel."

Celia wanted to say that it wasn't any fun unwrapping a gift you had wrapped yourself but caught herself in time. Instead, she tore away the wrapping paper, revealing a DVD. She showed it to Jake. "It's *Rebel Without a Cause*," she said, handing it over.

Jake skimmed the cover copy on the back of the DVD case. "Never heard of it."

"It's about a guy who's considered an outsider at his high school. He doesn't fit in. Maybe you remind your Secret Santa of James Dean."

"Who's James Dean?"

Celia wanted to clutch her heart. How could he not know who James Dean was? Did he never watch Turner Classic Movies on cable or go to the revival house in town? They were always showing great old movies made before even their parents were born!

"He was a movie star," Celia patiently exclaimed. "From the 1950s. He died really young in a car crash and only made three or four movies. *Rebel Without a Cause* is considered a classic."

Celia had bought Jake the movie because she thought he might identify with James Dean's character, who didn't really fit in, and who falls in love with the "nice" girl by the end of the movie. Hint, hint!

"Never heard of him," Jake said, tossing the DVD at Celia. "It sounds boring. You keep it. I never watch movies made before 1990."

A bummed Celia put the DVD back in her shoulder bag. She already owned a copy of the movie. Maybe she'd be able to get her money back at the video store.

Celia waited for Jake to notice what she was wearing, but he didn't say a word. He hardly even glanced at her.

Humph!

He also didn't ask if her Secret Santa had left her anything that morning.

"I called the bakery last night," she said, trying to make conversation. "Freddy told me you weren't working."

"I was at the mall Christmas shopping. I've still got a bunch of presents to buy."

"Shopping for anyone in particular?" Celia asked, hoping her question sounded casual. She wanted to hear Jake say he had been shopping for a gift for his Secret Santa! "Someone special?"

"Everyone on my Christmas list is special," Jake said, giving Celia a wink "Didn't you know that?"

Was Jake trying to tell her something? Celia

wondered. Send her a message? Was she one of the "someone specials" on his Christmas list? Could it be that Jake didn't want to spoil the surprise? That he wanted to wait until the night of the Christmas dance to reveal himself as her Secret Santa?

Or was she totally wrong and Jake *wasn't* her Secret Santa?

Shawna was walking to her American Literature class between third and fourth period when she saw Connor in the hallway. She decided she would give him a smile, as a way of showing him she was approachable. That she wasn't holding any sort of grudge from the day before. Hopefully, he'd wanted to come over and talk to her. Maybe they could patch things up.

But he completely ignored her.

Correction.

He didn't see her because his attention was focused elsewhere.

On his locker.

Where his Secret Santa had left him another gift.

It was hanging from the handle of his locker,

in a cute little stocking that had his name stitched on the front of it. *Stitched on the front of it!* That was *such* a girly thing to do!!!

As soon as Connor saw the stocking, he made a beeline for it, snatching it up with a huge smile on his face.

She didn't see what was inside the stocking because Connor continued on to his next class.

But she was livid.

Livid!!!

Only a girl would be leaving Connor such cute little packages.

A girl who was trying to steal her boyfriend!

She was still mad at lunchtime. When she got to the cafeteria, she could see Celia already sitting at their table. She instantly noticed her outfit.

"I'm impressed," she said, taking the seat next to her. "You look like you just stepped out of the pages of *Elle*."

"Thanks."

"I'm glad to see you're finally dressing like one of us," Amber said, slipping into the seat on the other side of Celia. "I'd wear what you have on."

But it wouldn't look as good on you as it does on

Celia, Shawna wanted to say. Instead, she began eating her salad, dipping the leaves into ranch dressing, listening to Amber talk about their plans for next week during the break. But she wasn't paying attention. Her eye kept darting across the cafeteria to where Connor and Simon were sitting. The Christmas stocking Connor had found was on the table, but what had been inside it?

"Shawna, is everything okay?" Celia asked. "You seem a million miles away."

"Shawna's preoccupied," Amber answered for her.

"With what?"

Amber speared a tomato from her salad and popped it into her mouth, grinning. "The girl who's after her boyfriend."

"What do you care if someone else is interested in Connor?" Celia asked. "I thought you wanted to date a senior."

Celia's comment hit a nerve and Shawna snapped her at her. "I'm not dating anyone new yet! Connor is still my boyfriend. I don't need some other girl giving him ideas about dumping me!"

Besides, Amber *wants to date a senior. Not me! I'm perfectly happy with Connor. But who knows?*

Maybe the other girls think Connor is fair game. Maybe some of them know about Amber's Secret Santa plan of switching the names. But how could they? Only Celia and Amber and I know about it, and we certainly didn't say anything to anyone else.

Unless . . .

"What's with the frown?" Mindy asked, sitting across from Shawna.

Bingo!

Did Mindy tell someone that I "wanted" to date a senior? Making Connor fair game for all the single girls at North Ridge High?

Shawna gasped as another thought popped into her mind.

Maybe Mindy didn't tell anyone because *she* was the one after Connor!

"I'm sensing tension," Mindy said, taking a sip of her diet Dr Pepper. "Talk to me. I'm a good listener."

And a good blabber, Shawna thought. She wouldn't tell Mindy her innermost secrets if her life depended on it. She decided to change the subject.

"Get another gift from your Secret Santa?" she asked.

"A bag of jawbreakers!" Mindy exclaimed as she bit into her chicken-salad sandwich. "Can you believe it? Do you know how hard those things are? I almost broke my jaw!"

That was one way to shut Mindy up, Shawna thought meanly. *Wire her mouth shut!*

"So what's going on at Connor's table, Shawna?" Mindy asked, opening up a bag of barbecued potato chips "You can't take your eyes off him. Missing your sweetie?"

"Shawna thinks Connor's Secret Santa is after him," Amber said, nibbling on a carrot. "From now until Friday night, she's not letting him out of her sight."

"But she's probably wrong," Celia jumped in, sensing that Connor's Secret Santa was a touchy subject. "After all, Shawna's Secret Santa is a guy, and he's not after her."

"A *cheap* guy," Amber sniffed. "What did he leave you this morning? A lollipop?"

"What's wrong with that?" Shawna shot back. "At least *my* Secret Santa is following the rules of the game."

"You're just jealous," Amber taunted, flaunting the beaded glass bracelet on her wrist, "because *my* Secret Santa leaves me gifts like this. I found it on my doorstep this morning. Isn't it fab?"

"It cost more than we're allowed to spend," Mindy said.

"And that's my problem because?" Amber demanded.

Mindy held her hands up in surrender. "I'm just saying!"

"Well don't say anything to anyone else," Amber warned.

Shawna knew that was exactly the wrong thing to say to Mindy. Because once she heard she wasn't supposed to say something to anyone else, she did.

And Amber knew that.

By the end of the day, the entire school would know that Amber had a Secret Santa who was buying her extravagant gifts.

Making all the other girls jealous.

Shawna could care less about Amber's Secret Santa. The only one she was concerned about was Connor's.

And she had just come up with a plan on how to figure out who it was!

David's cell phone was ringing.

He stared at it in surprise. He'd had the phone for six months and other than his parents and Froggy calling, it never rang.

But now he had a call!

And it was from a number he didn't recognize!

He scrambled to answer it before it stopped ringing, unclipping it from the holder on his belt. "Hello?" he said.

"It's me. Shawna."

"Hey, Shawna. What's up?"

And then he remembered what he had told Shawna the night before. About calling him if she needed a date for Friday night's dance. It couldn't be, could it? His heart began beating with excitement, and butterflies began doing somersaults in his stomach. He didn't even dare to hope! But then why would she be calling him?

He looked across the cafeteria to where she usually sat, but her seat was empty. "Where are you?"

"Meet me by the soda machine in five minutes. We'll talk there."

Before David could say anything else, Shawna hung up.

"What was that all about?" Froggy asked, flipping through the copy of the *Star Trek* novel David's Secret Santa had left for him that morning. David had already read it so he'd given it to Froggy. So far his Secret Santa has struck out twice, giving him gifts he already owned. Well, at least he was getting gifts. Froggy hadn't received anything yet from his Secret Santa. "Why's Shawna calling?"

David shrugged. "I don't know." He hadn't told Froggy about having had dinner at Shawna's house. He felt guilty for keeping a secret from his best friend, but he'd promised Shawna he wouldn't say anything. Besides, he and Froggy hadn't told each other who they'd picked from the Secret Santa bag. It was kind of the same thing. He got up from his seat. "But I'm about to find out."

Chapter Twelve

"I need your help," Shawna said when David joined her at the soda machine. She pretended she was trying to decide what kind of soda she wanted to buy, staring straight ahead at the brightly lit buttons. David stood at the soda machine next to her, pretending to do the same thing. "I need you to start hanging around Connor. Be his shadow. Follow his every move."

"And you want me to do this because . . ."

Shawna put some quarters into the soda machine and pressed a button. Seconds later a can of diet Pepsi rumbled out of the machine. "I want to find out who his Secret Santa is!" she exclaimed, opening the can of soda and taking a sip.

"And what's in it for me?" David asked.

Shawna nearly spit out the soda she was sipping. She couldn't believe what she was hearing. Guys always did what she wanted them to do, no questions asked!

"What do you mean what's in it for you?" She coughed.

David deposited his own quarters and then made a selection. A can of Sprite rumbled out of the machine and he popped it open. "You want something and I want something. I think we can make a deal."

"What kind of deal?" Shawna asked suspiciously although she had a feeling she knew *exactly* what kind of deal David wanted.

"I want to take you to Friday night's dance."

And she was right!

"No way!" Shawna hissed. "That's blackmail!"

David shrugged, taking a sip of his soda. "Then you'll have to find another spy. See you around." He started walking away.

"Wait!"

Shawna grabbed David by the shoulder and twirled him around. Obviously she had underestimated him. She figured because he had a crush on her, he'd do whatever she wanted, but that wasn't the case. She had to admire that to a certain degree. At the same time, she needed to get him to do what she wanted!

"How about a compromise?" she suggested.

"What kind of compromise?" he asked suspiciously.

"I won't go to the dance with you on Friday night, but I will go out with you on a date." She held up a finger. "One date. And I get to plan it. Those are the terms. Take it or leave it."

David's eyes lit up. "I'll take it!"

Shawna sighed. "I had a feeling you would say that."

"Does my Secret Santa think I'm seven years old?"

Connor showed Simon the latest gift his Secret Santa had left him. It was a Matchbox car and it was a Corvette.

"Cool!" Simon exclaimed, running the tiny toy car across the table. "I used to collect these when I was a kid."

"If you want it you can have it. I've got no use for it. You know how much I hate Corvettes."

"Sure you don't want to give it to Mr.

Ellingsworth as an early Christmas present? Butter him up before you give your oral presentation?"

"If I thought it would work, I would, but you know it won't."

"Yeah, you're right."

"My Secret Santa hasn't given me one good gift yet."

"Cheer up. There are still two days left. Maybe she'll get the next gift right. Otherwise you can always give it to me."

"You're definitely cleaning up. I'm starting to think my Secret Santa should be yours!"

Simon had begun to think the same thing. He didn't know who Connor's Secret Santa was, but he was intrigued by her. It had to be a girl. Only a girl would bake cookies, wrap such perfect packages, and have Connor's name stitched on a Christmas stocking. But her gifts were so off! It's like she knew nothing about Connor and *everything* about him. His own Secret Santa had been leaving him gifts that were *boring*! First there had been the horrible-smelling soap on a rope. Today's gift had been a pair of colored shoelaces for his sneakers!

Who could Connor's Secret Santa be?

He started looking around the cafeteria, trying to scope out all the girls. Had any of them been paying special attention to Connor lately? He didn't think so. Most of them knew Connor was dating Shawna and that meant he was off-limits. Still, some girls liked a challenge, and stealing Connor away from Shawna would be quite an accomplishment.

He noticed Lily and Noelle staring at his table. When they saw him staring back at them, they quickly looked away. Simon started to wonder. Lily had been at the toy store yesterday and he'd seen in her in the aisle with the Matchbox cars. Had she bought the Corvette? Could she be Connor's Secret Santa? If she was, did she have feelings for him that were more than friendly? Could they be romantic?

Simon didn't know why, but the thought of Lily liking Connor made him feel jealous.

As the cafeteria started clearing out for afternoon classes, Connor searched for Shawna, but he didn't see her anywhere. Amber and Celia weren't around either. They must have all left. Great. He didn't have any classes with Shawna that afternoon and after last class ended he was going to be at Ryan Grant's house wrapping toys before going to his part-time job. He probably wouldn't see Shawna until tomorrow.

He sighed. Girls! Who could figure them out? He couldn't understand why Shawna was so jealous of his Secret Santa. They were just gifts. And lousy ones at that!

Yet Shawna was acting like he was cheating on her!

Didn't she know him at all after all these months of dating?

Her attitude was starting to make him mad.

Did he really need this grief?

When he found himself getting mad at Shawna, he reminded himself of all the things he liked about her. The way she made him laugh. How he liked spending time with her. How he liked holding her close and how he especially liked kissing her.

Maybe she'd get back to normal once Secret Santas were revealed.

Speaking of Secret Santas, he had a gift to deliver to his.

He took a peek in his backpack to make sure

his latest gift was still there and then left the cafeteria.

"Simon's staring at us!" Lily hissed. "Why is he staring at us?"

"Maybe he's staring at us because we're staring at him," Noelle answered.

"Look away! Look away!"

"I'm looking away," Noelle said, picking up her tuna fish sandwich and taking a bite. "Calm down."

"How can I calm down?" Lily moaned. "I can't believe I got another Secret Santa gift wrong! Did you see what Connor did? He gave the Matchbox car to Simon. Why would he do that? I told you what I overheard yesterday. He loves Corvettes. I thought giving him a mini version would be a cute gift."

"Maybe he's outgrown toy cars. Or maybe he didn't get the cuteness angle of the gift. Guys aren't usually into cute. Unless it's a cute girl."

"Maybe."

"Here's a suggestion. Why don't you ditch that list and just wing it?"

"You could be right." Lily gazed around the cafeteria. "Hey! Take a look at Celia! She glammed it up today. Looks like she had the same idea as you."

Noelle checked out her competition and felt herself burning up with jealousy. How was she expected to compete against *that*?! "Who looks hotter? Me or her? Tell me the truth."

"I don't think I'm the right person to be asking that question."

"If you were a guy, who would you choose, me or her?" Noelle asked.

Lily raised an eyebrow. "In case you hadn't noticed, I'm not a guy."

"But if you were."

"Why don't you ask a real guy?" Lily grabbed Ryan's arm as he passed by their table with a lunch tray. "Like Ryan!"

He slid into the seat next to Lily. "Ask me what?"

"Who do you think looks hotter?" Lily asked. "Noelle or Celia?"

"Noelle," Ryan answered, taking a bite of his cheeseburger. "No question."

Lily looked at Noelle. "Satisfied?"

"If Charlie had to choose between me and

Celia, who do you think he would choose?" Noelle asked Ryan.

Ryan stopped chewing his cheeseburger. "What kind of crazy question is that?"

"A 'what if' question," Noelle shot back.

Ryan shook his head. "A 'what if' question is something like, 'If the world was going to come to an end tomorrow, what would you do?' Or, 'If you could have any sort of superpower, what would it be?'" Ryan opened a packet of ketchup and squirted it over his French fries. "Why are girls always competing with one another?"

"It's the way we're programmed," Lily said, snatching a French fry from Ryan's plate.

"Let's talk about something else," Ryan said. "How goes it with the Secret Santas?"

"Even though I've been messing things up with the person whose name I picked," Lily said, "my Secret Santa has been leaving me nice gifts. Yesterday it was a green silk hair ribbon and today I got a handmade picture frame. But that's nothing compared to Noelle. She has a *romantic* Secret Santa."

"Romantic? Really? Tell me more," Ryan urged, popping a handful of French fries into his mouth.

Noelle blushed. "There's nothing to say."

"There is too!" Lily exclaimed. "Yesterday her Secret Santa left her a Christmas angel and today he left her chocolate kisses with a note promising that his kisses would be just as sweet."

Ryan raised his eyebrows. "Mash notes from your Secret Santa. How very PG-13! Sounds like your Secret Santa might have a crush on you. That he might even *like* you!"

"Do you really think so?" Noelle asked. After all, Ryan was Charlie's brother and Ryan would know if Charlie was the romantic type. She had to ask the question. How could she not?! "Would Charlie do something like this?"

Ryan's face screwed up like he'd sucked a sour lemon. "Charlie?! You think *Charlie* is your Secret Santa? My brother is *not* your Secret Santa. Trust me, he doesn't have a romantic bone in his body!"

Before Noelle could explain why she felt Charlie was her Secret Santa, Ryan jumped out of his seat and stormed away from the table.

"What's his problem?" Lily asked.

Noelle shrugged. "Who knows?"

Lily snatched a final French fry off Ryan's plate. "I'm ready to go. You?"

"Ready."

As Lily and Noelle were leaving the cafeteria, they ran into Jason and Sonia, who were also leaving. As usual, their arms were wrapped around each other's waists.

"Ladies first," Jason said, allowing Noelle and Lily to walk through the door first.

"Thanks," Noelle said while Lily just stared blankly at Jason and his new girlfriend.

"Look what Jase gave me," Sonia said. She held out her wrist so Lily and Noelle could see the silver bracelet she was wearing. Dangling from it was a heart-shaped charm. "It's an early Christmas present."

Sonia rested her head on Jason's shoulder as she stared at Lily and Noelle, a smug smile twitching on her lips. She nestled closer to Jason so there was no mistaking her body language. The message was clear: *Jason is mine!*

"It's very pretty," Noelle said.

Lily didn't say anything. Instead, she just walked down the hallway as Noelle chased after her. "Lily! Wait!" She caught up with her. "Are you okay?"

Lily shook her head. "No, I'm not okay," she admitted. "It hurts seeing Jason with someone else." She sighed and closed her eyes. "But it doesn't hurt as much as it used to."

Noelle didn't say anything, but she took Lily's comments as a good sign. It meant her best friend's broken heart was healing.

Chapter Thirteen

Noelle wanted to scratch Celia's eyes out!

She couldn't believe what she was seeing.

Charlie — *her* Charlie — was kissing Celia!

At first she thought she was dreaming. That at any second she would open her eyes and poof! She'd be in her bedroom, snuggling under her sheets and quilt, listening to the buzz of her clock radio before she switched it over to music.

But this was no dream.

Charlie's lips were pressed against Celia's.

His arms were wrapped around her waist, pulling her against him.

And he was kissing her.

A kiss that a boyfriend gave to his girlfriend.

The way she had always imagined Charlie kissing her.

Then he pulled away from a stunned Celia and gave her a mischievous smile, pointing upward to the entrance of the living room. Noelle followed his finger. "You were standing under the mistletoe," he said. "That means I get a kiss."

Noelle wanted to scream and beat herself up. How could she have been so stupid? She knew that Mrs. Grant always hung up mistletoe. She should have scoped out the Grant house when she first arrived to help Ryan wrap presents for the Toys for Tots program and made sure she was strategically standing under a sprig of the green stuff so Charlie could kiss her.

But now the opportunity was gone because Charlie was on his way out the door, slipping into his navy blue peacoat, tossing a blue scarf around his neck, and pulling on a pair of black leather gloves. "I'm heading over to Party City for some balloons. Does anyone need anything?"

Just come back, Noelle thought. *Come back so this time I can be the one kissing you under the mistletoe!*

★   ★   ★

When Froggy saw Charlie kissing Celia under the mistletoe, he wanted to run across the living room and pull him off her.

If anyone should be kissing Celia, it should be him!

Charlie didn't need to kiss her. Mr. Hot Lips had kissed more girls than Froggy ever would.

Why hadn't he caught sight of the mistletoe? *Why? Why? Why?* It would have been the perfect opportunity for him to show Celia how much he cared about her.

One kiss could say so much!

But now the opportunity was gone. And none of the girls who had come to help wrap presents at Ryan's house were going to be standing anywhere near the mistletoe now that Charlie was gone. Sure, Connor and Simon and Ryan were still here, but Charlie was the one whose kiss mattered.

At least Celia seemed embarrassed by the kiss she'd gotten from Charlie. She was still blushing.

That was the one bright spot.

But Froggy still didn't like that Charlie had kissed her.

★   ★   ★

"Rein it in," Lily whispered to Noelle. "Rein it in."

"Rein what in?" Noelle asked as she unrolled a sheet of red wrapping paper decorated with gold bells on the living room carpet.

"You know what I'm talking about. The green-eyed monster. Could you be any more jealous of Celia? If looks could kill, she'd be dead meat by now!"

"Can you blame me? She got the kiss I've been waiting eight years for and it didn't even count! It was a mistletoe kiss. A freebie!"

"I wonder if his lips are as nice as the girls say they are," Lily said. "Maybe I should go ask Celia."

"Don't you dare!"

"Just teasing." Lily grabbed a roll of wrapping paper decorated with candy canes, a bag of colored bows, scissors, and a roll of scotch tape. "I'm going to go work next to Connor. Maybe if I talk with him I can figure out what his next Secret Santa gift should be."

"Good luck."

"Thanks. I have a feeling I'm going to need it."

★   ★   ★

As she predicted, Lily had a hard time trying to figure out Connor. Even though she was wrapping gifts right next to him, it seemed like they had nothing in common. Every time she tried to start a conversation, she'd get a few sentences out of him and that would be it.

Simon, on the other hand, wouldn't shut up! No matter what the topic was — movies, TV shows, music, videogames — he had something to say.

What was surprising was that it was something she wanted to hear.

Whether it was a discussion on who was more talented, Christina Aguilera or Gwen Stefani (they both agreed it was Gwen), the never-ending storyline on *Lost* (Answers! All they wanted were answers!), when *Smallville* would be heading to the big screen, no matter what she said, Simon had an opinion.

And it was usually one she agreed with.

"I'm lousy at wrapping presents," Simon said, comparing a box he had just wrapped to one Lily had finished wrapping. The Scotch tape on his box was all zigzagging and the taped ends of the box were all puffy.

"I don't think the kids will mind," Lily said as

she added her perfectly wrapped gift to the pile. "They're not going to be paying attention to the wrapping. They just want to see what's underneath it. They're going to be tearing like crazy."

"I can't believe all the packages we have to wrap," Simon said, surveying the rows of shopping bags in the living room.

"We'll get it all done."

"How come you sound so sure?"

"We have to get it done," Lily stated matter-of-factly. "Otherwise we're going to have a whole bunch of disappointed kids on Christmas morning and we can't let that happen!"

Simon started wrapping another box, but he was doing such a lousy job that Lily took over. "Here, let me show you," she said. "First, drape half of the wrapping paper over the package, then Scotch tape it into place and pull it tightly so the paper is smooth." She demonstrated as she explained. "Then fold over the rest of the paper. If it's a bit too long, you can fold it in half. Then Scotch-tape that side into place." She showed him how. "Now all you have to do is make little triangles at each end, fold them in, Scotch-tape the bottom half, then the top, and you're done!" Lily held out a perfectly wrapped package. "Ta-da!"

"You make it all look so easy," Simon said, taking the package out of Lily's hands. "Doesn't she, Connor?"

Connor looked up from the model airplane he was wrapping and shrugged. "I guess."

Lily wanted to scream! Why wasn't she connecting with Connor the way she was connecting with Simon? Argh! It would make shopping for him so much easier. Well, at least she knew what she was giving him tomorrow. She had remembered what Simon had said yesterday about the horror festival at the revival house and she was going to buy Connor two passes; that way, if he wanted to take someone with him — probably Shawna — he could.

Hopefully he'd like this gift. How could he not? He was a horror fan! But if he didn't, she'd only have one more chance to make things up to him before Friday night's dance.

If there was one thing Noelle knew Ryan loved to do at Christmas, it was sing along to "You're A Mean One, Mr. Grinch." But he hadn't when the song piped out of the CD player in the living room. In fact, now that she thought about it, he hadn't sung along with any of the Christmas carols when they were playing, and he usually did.

Even though he'd had a smile on his face when he'd let everyone into his house and showed them where all the toys and wrapping materials were, he was keeping to himself. Having known Ryan since the third grade, she knew when something was bothering him. Ryan was usually a people person. He loved talking and making people laugh. When he kept to himself, it meant there was a problem.

"Did you forget the words to the song?" she asked him, joining him in the dining room where he was wrapping a pile of Barbie dolls.

Ryan shrugged. "Guess I'm just not in the mood."

Noelle reached into a bag of bows and began adding them to the boxes Ryan had already wrapped. "How come?"

"Something's bothering me."

"What is it? Maybe it would help if you talked about it. You know you can tell me anything." And it was true. She and Ryan often turned to each other when they had a problem too difficult to solve on their own. "Remember the time in seventh grade when you borrowed Charlie's bike without asking and it got stolen? You didn't know what to do and I told you to be honest and tell him the truth."

"My parents made me sell my bike so he could buy a new one," Ryan reminded her.

"That's what happens when you don't ask permission!"

"Look who's talking!" Ryan laughed. "Remember when you borrowed your mother's gold earrings for Lily's fourteenth birthday party without asking and then you lost one?"

Noelle clutched her heart. "Don't remind me! That was one of the worst nights of my life. I knew if I didn't find that missing earring, I was dead."

"I helped you find it, didn't I?"

Noelle gave Ryan a smile. "Yes, you did. You helped me search Lily's backyard with a flashlight for over two hours. It was pitch-black but you didn't give up. You were there when I needed you. So come on," she urged. "Tell me what's wrong."

Ryan shook his head. "I don't think you're going to want to hear this."

"Will you *please* just tell me?"

Ryan sighed. "Can I give you some advice?"

"Advice? What kind of advice?"

"Advice that I think you need."

Noelle pushed aside a pile of gifts at the dining room table and sat herself down in a chair, propping her chin in her hand. "You've intrigued me. I'm dying to hear what you have to say, Dr. Grant."

Ryan twirled a piece of ribbon around his finger, not looking at Noelle. "I know you have a crush on Charlie, but he's only going to hurt you. My brother's not ready to commit to one girl. He likes playing the field. He always thinks that someone better is going to come along. That's why he's always going from girlfriend to girlfriend. I don't want you to wind up being just another one of Charlie's exes."

Noelle couldn't believe what she was hearing. First, was her crush on Charlie that obvious that Ryan was able to notice it? And if Ryan was able to notice, who else had? Second, who was Ryan to be giving her advice about her love life? Who she decided to crush on was her own business, nobody else's. Third, how dare he say what he did about Charlie!

An angry Noelle bolted out of her seat. She

jumped up so fast, the chair fell to the hardwood floor with a loud crash, getting the attention of everyone who was wrapping toys. All eyes were now focused on her and Ryan. "I can't believe you would say such horrible things about your own brother!"

"What I said isn't horrible," Ryan stated, gazing into Noelle's eyes. "It's the truth."

Noelle shook her head. "No, it isn't. It's mean and malicious."

Ryan threw his hands up in the air. "Why would I be mean and malicious? Why would I lie?"

Noelle didn't know where the words came from. They just spewed out of her. "Because you're jealous!"

"Jealous?" Ryan laughed in disbelief. "*I'm* jealous?"

Noelle nodded. "That's right. You're jealous because girls aren't interested in you the way they're interested in Charlie."

"If girls aren't interested in me," Ryan shot back, "it's because none of them will give me a chance! They're all blinded by the great Charlie Grant. They all think he's so perfect with his white teeth, shiny hair, and muscles. Well, guess what? Charlie's not so great! He's not perfect! I should know because I live with him! You don't. So if I say my brother's a player, you should give me a little credit and listen to me."

"I don't want to listen to you and you know what? I don't have to!" Noelle shouted. "I'm going home!"

And with those final words, Noelle stormed out of Ryan's house.

Chapter Fourteen

After Noelle left, there was complete silence. Everyone stopped talking. Even the CD player was silent.

"I better make sure she's okay," Lily said, breaking the silence and hurrying after Noelle. "You can handle the rest, right, Ryan?"

Lily didn't wait for an answer as she struggled into her coat and raced out the front door.

Simon checked his watch. "I've got to get to work."

"Me too," Connor piped up, checking his own watch.

And then they were gone.

"Looks like it's just us," Ryan said to Celia and Froggy as he filled a shopping bag with wrapped packages.

"Actually, I have to get to work myself," Froggy said.

"And I have to get home," Celia quickly added.

"But I could come by tomorrow," Froggy offered.

"That's okay," Ryan said. "We wrapped a lot and my folks can help me finish up the rest. We're in good shape."

Ryan walked Froggy and Celia to the front door. "Thanks for all your help. I'll see you at school tomorrow."

As Froggy and Celia stepped out onto the front porch, they could see it had started snowing.

"Ooooh!" Celia exclaimed excitedly as she watched big white flakes fall to the ground. "We're going to have a white Christmas!"

As they walked down the darkened streets past houses lit with colorful Christmas lights, Froggy decided to ask Celia a question. "Did you really need to get home?"

Celia shook her head. "No."

"Then why didn't you stay? Ryan still had a lot of wrapping to do."

"I didn't want to risk running into Charlie again."

"How come? Afraid of those hot lips?"

Celia made a face. "I can't stand guys who are full of themselves and Charlie Grant is full of himself. Besides, his kiss wasn't that great."

Celia's words were music to Froggy's ears. *She hadn't liked Charlie's kiss!*

"I bet if Noelle had been standing under that mistletoe, she would disagree with you," Froggy said.

"Noelle's got it pretty bad for Charlie. I hope she doesn't get hurt. Guys like Charlie are bad news."

"Sounds like you've gone out with a Charlie yourself," Froggy said. Why should he be surprised if she had? Celia was beautiful. She'd probably gone on lots of dates when she lived in California and left behind a string of broken hearts.

"No, but every high school has that type. You know, Mr. Gorgeous. Mr. Popularity who all the girls swoon over. Ours was named Sawyer Chandler. He could have been a movie star, he was so good-looking. And he knew it! Girls were always throwing themselves at him, including my best friend, Crishell."

"Did he break her heart?" Froggy asked as

they reached the entrance of the town park and began walking down a winding path. Snowbanks were building and everything was covered with white. A group of ten-year-old girls were building a snowman and a bunch of boys were carrying their sleds to the top of the park's hill.

"Big time. Crishell's a romantic, so on Valentine's Day she made all these plans for them. Tickets to a play, reservations at a fancy restaurant. Even flowers and chocolates!"

"So what went wrong?"

"The creep sent her a text message on Valentine's Day while she was waiting for him to show up at the theater," Celia said. "He said he'd met someone else that day — *that same day* — and there was an instant chemistry between them. He said he couldn't resist it."

"What a jerk!"

"I know! He knew Crishell was waiting for him at the theater. He could have at least gone out on one last date with her and then broken up with her the next day. It would have hurt, but it wouldn't have hurt as much as being by yourself on Valentine's Day, standing with a heart-shaped box of chocolates and flowers, watching other couples make kissy-face at each other!"

Celia looked up at the sky. "The snow is coming down harder."

Froggy scooped up a handful of snow from a park bench and molded it into a snowball. "It's sticking," he said, tossing the snowball from one hand to the other.

Celia started making a snowball of her own. "I've never been around snow before," she said. "All my life I've lived in California." She showed Froggy her snowball, a mischievous glint in her eye. "What am I supposed to do with this now?"

"I think you know what you're supposed to do with it," Froggy said, backing away. "But I should warn you. I'm a pretty good snowball thrower. So if you throw one at me, I'm going to throw one back at you!"

"You mean like this?" Celia shrieked, throwing her snowball at Froggy and hitting him in the middle of his chest.

"Yes!" Froggy exclaimed, tossing his own snowball and hitting Celia in the shoulder as he ducked behind a huge oak tree.

Within seconds they were scooping snow off the ground and tossing snowballs back and forth at each other. Deciding to outfox Celia, Froggy ducked behind a low hedge and began crawling in the direction where she was hiding. When he was inches away from her, he made a handful of snowballs and tucked them in the crook of his arm. Then he jumped up from behind the hedge with a loud yell, tossing the snowballs at a surprised Celia.

"You rat!" Celia laughed, whirling around and trying to fend off the snowballs with her hands as she was pelted. She scooped up a handful of snow and raced toward Froggy, who had used up all his snowballs, crashing into him. Together they fell backward into a snowbank.

"Hey! We can make snow angels!" Celia exclaimed excitedly, moving her arms up and down and her legs from side to side.

Froggy turned his head to look at Celia. He couldn't believe how much fun she was having in the snow. She didn't care that her clothes were getting soaking wet. She was having a great time. Her eyes were lit up and she was laughing and smiling. Their faces were so close together that all he wanted to do was lean over and kiss her. He couldn't take his eyes off her lips. They were so soft and pink. He wanted to kiss her *so* badly, but this wasn't some fairy tale where the ugly frog turns into Prince Charming after getting a kiss from the beautiful girl. This was real life and in real life, guys like him did *not* kiss girls like Celia.

No matter how badly they wanted to!

"How come you're looking at me so funny?" Celia asked, tossing a handful of snow in Froggy's face.

The handful of snow was like a splash of cold water, snapping Froggy back into reality. He jumped to his feet and then pulled Celia off the ground.

"I'm late for work," he said, glancing at his watch and dusting snow off his pants and jacket. "I'll see you at school tomorrow. Bye!"

And then Froggy rushed out of the park without even another look at Celia.

Celia stared at a departing Freddy in confusion. What had just happened? They had been having such a nice time and then all of a sudden Freddy ran off like he was *afraid* of her. Why would Freddy be afraid of her?

Seconds later a cold wind cut through Celia and she started shivering in her wet clothes. All thoughts of Freddy left her mind as she hurried home, obsessed with thoughts of a warm bubble bath, her fuzzy pajamas, and a hot cup of cocoa.

David was trying to make himself invisible.

He was sitting at a corner table at Vincinzi's, an Italian restaurant where Connor worked as a busboy, hiding behind a huge menu. He was pretty sure Connor didn't know who he was — to a certain degree, guys who were considered nerds *were* invisible — but he didn't want to take a chance.

He'd been following Connor around since after school. First he'd followed him to Ryan Grant's house, and then he'd followed him here. Waiting for him to leave Ryan's hadn't been fun. Even wearing a heavy sweater, down-filled parka, gloves, scarf, hat, and snow boots, it was cold outside. And then it had started snowing. David was practically a snowman by the time Connor had left. Luckily Connor had come straight to work, and David had a chance to warm himself up while continuing to spy for Shawna.

David watched as Connor went from table to table, clearing away dishes, refilling water glasses, and bringing out breadbaskets. Practically every table he went to had a girl from their high school. David wondered if they were here because the food was so good or if it was because of Connor.

David couldn't help but feel jealous as he stared at Connor. The guy was a hottie with muscles that didn't quit, hair made for a shampoo commercial, and a killer smile. Not to mention the cleft in his chin and his two dimples! David, on the other hand, was a string bean with braces and carrot-red hair that was always a frizzy mess, like he had just stuck his finger in an electric socket. Oh, and no cleft in his chin or dimples, but occasional zits! What would it be like to be as handsome as Connor and always have girls throwing themselves at you? Could you get tired of it? David didn't think he would.

David ducked back behind his menu and wondered how long he'd be able to sit at his table. He had enough money to order an entrée, but that was it. He'd take his time eating, but he really wasn't looking forward to positioning himself outside the restaurant for hours.

The only thought that kept him going, though, was Shawna and the date they were going to have.

If he discovered who Connor's Secret Santa was, Shawna would be in his debt.

Maybe she'd agree to a second date.

Or even give him a kiss!

David's eyes roamed around the restaurant and stopped when they came to Connor's workstation. Patty Suskind, a pretty redhead, was opening a drawer where the silverware was kept and leaving behind a small wrapped present.

Yes!

Success!

David pulled out his cell phone and dialed Shawna's number. When she answered her cell phone, he told her that he'd discovered who Connor's Secret Santa was.

"Where are you?" she asked.

"Vincinzi's."

"I'll be right there," Shawna said, her voice filled with determination. David knew what that meant. Shawna was ready for a confrontation! He hoped Patty hadn't ordered anything with tomato sauce. She was wearing a snow-white sweater, and he had a feeling things might get a little *messy* once Shawna arrived. That sweater might not be snow-white once Shawna got through with Patty!

David's eyes returned to Connor's workstation and almost fell out.

Jenna Martindale was leaving a present for Connor.

Five minutes later, Faye Bennett was doing the same thing.

And Olga Nivinson.

And Vicky Stevens!

Uh-oh.

He had the feeling he'd just made a mistake.

A huge one.

Which girl was Connor's Secret Santa?

They couldn't all be.

And what was he going to tell Shawna?

Shawna!

David felt the blood rush out of his face. She was going to be here any second, ready for a fight with Patty but there was a good chance that Patty *wasn't* Connor's Secret Santa. That it was one of the other girls.

David jumped out of his seat and struggled back into his parka, hurrying out of the restaurant. He'd just gotten outside when Shawna came storming down the street.

"Where is she?" Shawna demanded. "I'm going to yank every red hair out of her head!"

"We have a little bit of a problem," David said, grabbing Shawna by the arm and steering her away from the entrance of the restaurant.

"What do you think you're doing?" Shawna asked, her voice dripping with ice. She stared down at the hand holding her arm and David instantly let go, amazed at the power of Shawna's glare.

"Sorry," David said meekly, smoothing out the wrinkled fabric.

"What's the problem?" Shawna asked, snatching her arm away.

David fidgeted, not sure how to explain things because he had the feeling Shawna was going to get mad at him. After all, he'd called to tell her Patty was Connor's Secret Santa and now he wasn't sure!

"Come on!" Shawna demanded, snapping her fingers. "Spit it out! I haven't got all night!"

"AfterPattyleftagiftforConnorsodidJennaMar tindaleandacoupleofothergirls," David said in a rush, not pausing to take a breath.

"Then why did you call me?" Shawna screeched.

"The other girls didn't leave their gifts until after I called you," David explained, handing over a list of names. "There's no way of figuring out which one is Connor's Secret Santa. At least not yet."

"How do you know all these girls by name?" Shawna asked, looking over the list. "I don't even know all of them."

David blushed. "Guys like me always notice pretty girls like you."

Shawna rolled her eyes. "You've got your date. You don't have to butter me up."

"But it's the truth! You're gorgeous." David pointed to the list. "What do you want to do about these girls?"

Shawna crumpled the list. "I bet Connor is going to meet one of them for a date after his shift ends." She pulled David into the alley next to the restaurant. "Well, we're going to wait until he gets off work and then we're going to follow him!"

"But that could take hours!" David exclaimed. "And it's cold!"

"So?"

"It's cold!" David repeated. "*Freezing* cold! And it's still snowing!"

Shawna crossed her arms over her chest. "Do you want that date or not?"

Of course he did!

"Yes," he answered. "You know I do!"

"Then we're waiting!" Shawna snapped.

One hour later David and Shawna were as cold as two Popsicles. They were both covered with snow, stomping their feet and moving around in circles as a way of keeping themselves warm, still waiting for Connor to leave work.

David's teeth were chattering. "M-m-maybe he's working a d-d-double shift. M-m-maybe we s-s-should throw in the t-t-towel for t-t-tonight and t-t-then —"

"Shh!" Shawna hissed, cutting David off as she peeked around the side of the alley. "Connor's coming out of the restaurant." She gasped. "And he's not alone! He's heading this way with a girl!"

"If he looks this way, he'll see us!" David pointed out. "We have to hide!"

"Where?" Shawna asked in a panic. "Where?"

David looked around. The only hiding space in the alley was the restaurant's garbage dumpster. "In there."

"Are you crazy?"

"Do you want to get caught?"

"No."

David lifted the lid of the dumpster. "Then jump inside."

"Ewww! It smells gross!" Shawna complained as she climbed into the dumpster. David joined her seconds later, lowering the lid so they could peek outside.

"Did you get to see who it was?" David asked, holding his nose. The dumpster smelled bad!

"No," Shawna gasped, covering her nose with her hand. "I can't breathe!"

They peeked out of the dumpster as Connor walked by alone.

"What happened to the girl?" Shawna asked.

They could hear a car engine starting.

"It was probably a customer leaving the restaurant the same time as Connor," David said.

"You're probably right," Shawna agreed.

David and Shawna were both so focused on Connor that they didn't hear the sound of footsteps coming down the alley. Seconds later the lid of the dumpster was lifted and a pile of garbage was tossed in, drenching them with everything from vegetable skins to tomato sauce, chicken skins, and leftover pasta.

"Groossssssssssssss!" Shawna screamed, jumping out of the dumpster and nearly giving the old

Italian busboy holding an empty trash can a heart attack.

"Whassa matter with you?" he demanded in a thick accent, clutching his chest. "Why you hiding inna there?"

"Can you help me out, Shawna?" David asked, holding out a hand and taking deep breaths of air. Shawna reached out and started to pull, but David couldn't get enough traction. Instead, he slid back into the dumpster, pulling Shawna in with him and headfirst into a pile of garbage.

"You idiot!" she shrieked, pulling broken eggshells out of her hair. "Look what you've done!"

"What *I've* done?" David snapped, losing all patience. "You're the one who has me spying on your boyfriend, although if you really trusted him, you wouldn't be spying on him!"

Shawna threw a cantaloupe rind at David. "I do trust Connor! I don't trust those she-wolves we go to school with!"

"If you trusted Connor you'd know that he would never cheat on you. I know if you were *my* girlfriend, I'd never cheat on you."

"But I'm *not* your girlfriend. I'm Connor's," Shawna said, climbing back out of the dumpster.

When she got out, she turned back to David. "I'm going home to get out of these horrible clothes, but you're going keep following Connor."

"But I'm a mess!" David wailed.

"Too bad! You're working for me, remember? Unless you want to give up that date I agreed to."

There was *no way* David was giving up that date. Not after everything he had already been through! He held his hand out to the old Italian busboy, who helped pull him out.

"I'll let you know what I find out," David said, hurrying out of the alley. He was a freezing, smelly mess, but so was Shawna. They finally had something in common!

Chapter Fifteen

The first thing Noelle loved to do when she woke up after a big snowstorm was rush to her bedroom window and look outside. But not this morning. After turning off the buzzer of her alarm and switching it to the radio — "Suddenly I See," the opening song from her favorite movie, *The Devil Wears Prada,* was playing — she flopped back against her pillows, snuggling against the toasty warmth of her comforter. She didn't want to get up. All she wanted to do was close her eyes and go back to sleep. She'd been having *such* a nice dream. Charlie had been kissing her and telling her she was the only girl for him. He'd only gone out with all those other girls because he wanted to make her jealous, he told her as he wrapped his arms around her and pulled her close. She was the *only* girl for him.

Noelle smiled, stretching her arms as she remembered the way Charlie had kissed her. His dream kiss had been nice, but she was sure a real kiss from him would be *so* much better.

Hopefully she'd be getting that real kiss tomorrow night.

Knowing she needed to get up, she hopped out of bed. The hardwood floor was icy cold and she hurriedly slipped her feet into a pair of fleece-lined slippers. Pushing the tangled mess that was her hair out of her face, she stifled a yawn and walked over to the window, pulling the curtains back as she pressed her face to the glass.

She gasped with delight. It was a winter wonderland in her front yard. Everywhere she looked, there was smooth white snow. It was like everything had been covered with vanilla frosting. She loved snow when it first fell — all light and fluffy and pretty — but hated when it became gray and slushy and frozen a couple of days later. She was stifling a yawn with one hand, wondering if she had time to slip back into bed for another fifteen minutes, when she saw something in the corner of her front yard. Was that a snowman? She pressed her face closer to the cold frosted glass and squealed with glee. It was! But who could have built it?

Noelle grabbed a pair of jeans off the floor and pulled them on over her pajama bottoms. Then she raced downstairs and threw on her overcoat and gloves. She stuffed her hair under a knit hat, wrapped a scarf around her neck, and pulled on her snow boots. Then she raced outside into the freezing morning and the waiting snowman.

When she got closer, she could see the snowman was holding something in the hand she couldn't see from her bedroom window. It was a bouquet of balloons. A rainbow of bright colors — red, green, yellow, blue, pink, and orange — danced in the morning air. Pinned to the front of the snowman's chest was a note: *Being around you always lifts me up.*

Noelle's heart turned to mush. The gift was *so* sweet. It had to be from Charlie. It just had to! Hadn't he said yesterday afternoon that he had to buy some balloons? He was giving her a clue. He *wanted* her to know that he was her Secret Santa. Why else would he have mentioned the balloons?

At that moment, the front door of the Grant house opened and Charlie came walking out. Noelle's first instinct was to run across the yard and throw herself in his arms, telling him how much she loved his gift. Then she remembered how she was dressed and her second instinct was to run and hide. Even though she was covered from head to toe, underneath she was a mess. And she hadn't even brushed her teeth. She still had morning breath!

"Hey, Noelle!" Charlie called. "Couldn't wait to build a snowman?"

"Someone built him for me," Noelle said. "And look." She pointed to the colorful bouquet. "They left balloons too."

"Those look like they came from Party City."

"Really?" Noelle's heart began pounding with excitement. Charlie had gone to Party City yesterday afternoon to buy balloons. He had told them that before leaving. Was he giving her a clue? What should she say next? Did he want her to ask him if he'd bought balloons yesterday afternoon? Or ask him how he knew these balloons were from Party City? Would that spoil the surprise? Should she mention the note?

A car horn honked, jarring Noelle from her

thoughts. She looked at the curb and saw a red SUV. She couldn't see who was behind the steering wheel, but the shadow of the driver looked very thin and girly. Grrrr!

"Gotta go," Charlie said. "There's my ride."

Before she could say anything else, Noelle watched as Charlie hurried down the front walk and jumped into the SUV. He gave her a final wave before the car pulled away.

Noelle watched as the SUV disappeared. Then turned back to the snowman. So what if the driver was female? Charlie had made her this snowman. He'd bought her the balloons. He might be with another girl now, but tomorrow night, after Secret Santas were revealed, he would be hers!

An hour later Noelle was getting ready to leave for school when her cell phone rang. She looked at the screen and saw the call was from Lily.

"What's up?" she asked, pressing the phone against her ear.

"You've got to help me!" Lily wailed, panic in her voice.

"With what?"

"I'm at school and I forgot to bring Connor's latest Secret Santa gift in. I don't have time to run home and get it. I've got an early class. Could you swing by my house and pick it up? My mom knows you're coming. All you have to do is figure out a way to leave it for Connor without being seen."

"Sure. Not a prob. See you at lunch."

Before heading over to Lily's to pick up Connor's Secret Santa gift, Noelle had Charlie's latest gift to deliver. She didn't have to make sure she wasn't seen since all the Grants were already gone. Mr. and Mrs. Grant had left the house minutes after Charlie had and Ryan was in the same early class as Lily.

Ryan. Noelle was still mad at him, but she wasn't as mad as she had been yesterday afternoon. She was cooling off. Still, she wasn't sure what she was going to do or say the next time she saw him. Things might be a little chilly between them. But they'd had fights before and they always managed to patch things up.

Noelle put her hand into her coat pocket and pulled out Charlie's latest gift. Today it was something simple. A pack of Doublemint, Charlie's favorite chewing gum. The note she had written said: *I love fresh, minty kisses so be sure to chew this tomorrow night!*

Noelle was a little unsure of the note. She'd never been so forward with a guy. Usually she let them make the first move. But sometimes you had to be direct to get what you wanted.

And she wanted a kiss from Charlie!

Before she could change her mind, she slipped the wrapped pack of gum into the Grants' locked mailbox. Then she hurried over to Lily's house, where Mrs. Norris was waiting for her with a small wrapped box. Noelle knew it contained two passes to GORE-A-RAMA, the horror festival at the revival house next month. Ick!

When she arrived at school, Noelle went to her locker and got her books for her morning classes. Then she decided to leave Connor his Secret Santa gift. Knowing that American History was his first class on Thursday mornings, Noelle slipped into the classroom and left Lily's gift on top of his desk. Then she slipped out of the empty classroom without anyone seeing her. Mission accomplished!

★　　★　　★

Simon couldn't believe what he was seeing.

Noelle Kramer was Connor's Secret Santa?

He had been so sure it was Lily!

Simon had been the first person to arrive for his American History class. As he was getting ready to open the door, he saw Noelle through the pane of glass in the door, which confused him. Noelle wasn't in his American History class. What was she doing inside the classroom? He pressed his face to the pane of glass and gasped.

She was leaving a gift on top of Connor's desk!

Not wanting to be seen, Simon had ducked away. When Noelle left the classroom seconds later, he had raced inside to Connor's desk, staring at the wrapped gift. On top of it was a note: *To Connor, Merry Xmas! Your Secret Santa*

Simon was blown away. He'd been so sure that Lily was Connor's Secret Santa, but she wasn't.

It was Noelle.

As he thought about it, the pieces all fell into place. Lily and Noelle were best friends. When Noelle had picked Connor's name, she had probably asked Lily to help her figure out what she should buy for Connor as gifts. That was why

Lily was always hanging around Connor and asking him questions.

She was acting on Noelle's behalf and reporting back to her.

Noelle was the one he had so much in common with, not Lily.

That meant the feelings he was starting to develop for Lily really hadn't been for *Lily*.

They had been for Noelle!

Simon had never thought of Noelle romantically before, but now that he knew the truth, he was going to have to do something about it!

A bouquet of purple daisies was waiting on Celia's desk in Anatomy and Physiology.

"Look!" she exclaimed to Froggy, holding out the bouquet. "Aren't they pretty?"

Froggy barely glanced up from the Robert Jordan novel he was reading. "Uh-huh."

"They're from my Secret Santa," Celia said, fingering the purple petals. "Wasn't that thoughtful of him? You know, when a guy sends a girl flowers, it means he likes her."

Froggy put down his book. Something in

Celia's tone of voice made him nervous. He didn't know what it was, but he had a feeling. A bad feeling. "How do you know your Secret Santa is a guy?"

Celia gave Froggy a coy smile. "I just do. A girl always knows when a guy is interested in her."

For a second, Froggy panicked. What did that smile mean? Did Celia know he was her Secret Santa? Was she trying to let him know that she knew? No, that was impossible. There was no way she could know. Jake was the one getting to know Celia with each passing day, not him. And Jake was the one telling him everything he found out about her. He knew that he should be the one getting to know Celia on his own instead of hiding behind Jake. He wished he had the courage to tell her how he really felt.

He'd come close last night.

Very close.

But he'd been afraid.

What if he had kissed Celia? What then?

Would she have kissed him back?

Yeah, right.

Her face would have screwed up like she'd sucked a sour lemon and she would have said,

"Ewww! What do you think you're doing kissing me?"

What was going to happen tomorrow night when Celia found out he was her Secret Santa and not the handsome hunk she was imagining? He could just see the expression on her face. First there would be shock, then horror and disbelief. She would try hard not to let him see what she was really feeling inside — because he knew Celia wasn't the type of person to hurt anyone's feelings — but before she could hide those feelings, they would creep out. Just for a second.

But a second was all it would take for him to know he and Celia weren't meant to be together.

"Was it busy at the bakery last night?" Celia asked.

"Super busy."

"Was Jake working?"

"Yeah."

"Do you guys work together a lot?" Celia asked. "What days isn't he working and when he's not working do you know what he likes to do for fun? Where does he usually hang out?"

Froggy shrugged. "I don't have a clue."

"You must know! Come on!" Celia urged. "Tell me something about Jake that I don't know."

"Why all the questions about Jake?" Froggy asked.

Celia looked around the lab, almost like she was making sure she wouldn't be overhead. "Can I tell you a secret?"

"Sure."

"Promise not to tell?"

"Promise."

Celia leaned in close to Froggy. He could smell the light floral scent of her perfume and the strawberry shampoo she used on her hair. It was pure heaven!

"I have a crush on Jake," she whispered into Froggy's ear. "I've had it for a while, and I'm pretty sure he's my Secret Santa!"

Heaven quickly turned to hell. Celia's words were like an ice pick thrust into Froggy's heart. Celia liked *Jake*? No, he couldn't have heard her correctly. It had to be a mistake.

"You like *Jake*?" Froggy whispered back, his voice barely a croak.

Celia's blue eyes glittered with excitement. "Yes!"

It wasn't a mistake.

Well, why wasn't he surprised? Jake was a bad boy, a rebel, the type of guy most girls usually fell for.

They never fell in love with the four-eyed nerd.

"It's all I can do not to tell Jake that I know he's my Secret Santa," Celia confessed, explaining to Froggy how she had figured it out. "What should I do?"

Froggy swallowed over the lump in his throat, forcing his words out. "Don't say anything. You should wait until the dance tomorrow night when everything will be perfect and romantic and Secret Santas are revealed."

"You think?"

"Absolutely," Froggy said with a forced smile, trying to look cheerful. The last thing he wanted to do was smile. He wanted to cry. He had lost Celia, but had he ever really had her? No. It had all been a dream, and deep down he knew that she was never going to be his. "Who knows what other surprises your Secret Santa might have in store for you? You wouldn't want to ruin them, would you?"

"I guess not," Celia said.

"Trust me on this. Tomorrow night is going to be everything you dreamed it would be. And more!"

Celia fidgeted through most of Anatomy and Physiology, barely listening to Mr. Seleski's lecture or taking notes. She constantly kept checking the time on her watch, waiting for the next bell to ring.

All she could think about was Jake!

It was going to be hard when she saw him next period in Art class. She wanted to tell him that she knew he was her Secret Santa and that she loved, loved, loved all the gifts he had gotten her, especially the daisies.

Who knew Jake could be so romantic?

As much as she wanted to throw her arms around him and give him a hug — and definitely a kiss! — she wouldn't. She couldn't! If she did, she would spoil the surprise. Freddy was right. She couldn't let Jake know that she knew he was her Secret Santa. She was going to have to keep pretending she didn't know who her Secret Santa was and wait until tomorrow night's dance for Jake to reveal himself to her.

Then she could hug and kiss him as much as she wanted!

Finally the bell for next period rang. Celia threw everything into her backpack, said a quick good-bye to Freddy, and raced out of the classroom, eager to get to Art class. Even though she couldn't let Jake know she had figured out he was her Secret Santa, she could let him know how much she loved her purple daisies.

And how she couldn't wait to thank her Secret Santa at Friday night's dance!

Celia didn't expect Jake to be in Art class when she got there. He always showed up right under the wire. Since she was the first one in class, she left Jake's latest Secret Santa gift on his desk. She hoped he liked this one. She'd gotten him a pair of fingerless gloves that he could wear when riding his motorcycle. Actually, she'd bought a pair of black knit gloves and cut the fingers off herself!

After taking her seat, she kept her eyes glued on the classroom door, waiting for him to stroll in at the last minute the way he usually did, all attitude.

But when the bell rang for class to begin, there was still no Jake.

Mr. Catini closed the classroom door and Celia waited for Jake to open it

But he didn't.

"Does anyone know where our friend Mr. Morrisey is?" Mr. Catini asked as he began taking attendance.

"He's out sick today," Sheila Windsor called out. "I was in the attendance office when his mother called in."

Celia couldn't believe what she was hearing.

Out sick?!

Jake was out sick?

He couldn't be!

Because if he was, then that meant Jake *wasn't* her Secret Santa.

He couldn't have left her the purple daisies this morning.

And if he hadn't left her the daisies, then that meant he *hadn't* been the one leaving her gifts all week.

So if Jake wasn't her Secret Santa, then who was?

Chapter Sixteen

Noelle and Lily were in the cafeteria, eating their lunch. From the second she had sat down, Noelle had felt a pair of eyes staring at her. At first she couldn't figure out who it was. The cafeteria was filled with students and everyone was busy talking and laughing, walking to their tables with filled lunch trays. She'd taken a look around, but didn't notice anyone looking her way, so she'd gone back to eating her lunch.

But then she *felt* it. She got the sense that someone was looking at her. Almost like they were *studying* her. It creeped her out for a little bit, but then she scolded herself for being so silly. This wasn't some slasher movie!

She casually took another look around the

cafeteria, pretending like she was looking for someone, and then her eyes fell on Simon and Connor's table.

She was about to look away when she realized something.

Simon was the one staring at her.

Why would Simon be staring at her?

When he caught her looking at him, their eyes locked and he gave her a smile. The intensity of his gaze spooked her. It was almost like he was trying to get into her mind! She smiled back and quickly returned to eating her lunch, but seconds later she peeked over her shoulder. She couldn't help herself. *Had* Simon been the one staring at her?

Yes!

He was!

Because he was *still* staring at her.

And still smiling at her.

"Why is Simon smiling at me?" she asked Lily.

"Huh?" Lily asked, grappling with chopsticks as she tried to tackle that day's special, chicken chow mein.

"Simon," Noelle said. "He keeps smiling at me. But there's something off about his smile."

Lily peeked over her shoulder. "What do you mean *off*?"

"Don't look!" Noelle hissed.

Lily sighed. "How am I supposed to know if his smile is off unless I see it?"

"You don't have to be so obvious! Couldn't you have pretended you were looking at someone else?"

"Like Connor? That's what I was doing!" Lily pouted. "Oh, shoot! Connor is leaving!"

"So what do you think?"

"About what?" Lily asked, her eyes following Connor as he left the cafeteria.

"Simon!"

"It's a smile!" Lily exclaimed.

Noelle shook her head. "No, it isn't. It's almost like he knows a secret of mine, and he's telling me he knows, but he's not going to tell anybody else."

"How could Simon possibly know any of your secrets?" Lily asked. "You don't have any!"

"Then why does he keep smiling at me?"

Lily shrugged, abandoning her chopsticks for a fork and digging into her lunch. "I don't know. Maybe he just came from the dentist and the dentist gave him laughing gas."

"I don't like it," Noelle said. "Until today,

Simon didn't know I existed. Now, all of a sudden, he's smiling at me?"

"Simon's a hottie! Who cares why he's smiling at you? Just enjoy it!"

"In case you've forgotten, I'm interested in another hottie. Plus, I don't want Amber thinking I'm after her boyfriend."

"Are they still a couple?" Lily asked, opening a can of diet 7-Up.

"I don't know. Aren't they?"

"I haven't seen them together much lately."

"Maybe Amber's moved on."

"Or maybe Simon's decided to move on," Lily said, popping a straw into her can of soda and taking a sip. "To you!"

Connor was on his way to gym class when he got the sense he was being followed. He turned around to see who was behind him, but the corridor was empty. He retraced his steps, looking down two intersecting hallways, but no one was there.

Still, he couldn't shake the feeling that someone had been walking behind him. He'd had the same feeling the night before when he left work but had ignored it, hurrying to get home because it was so cold out.

Hmmm. Very strange.

He had to be imagining things.

After all, who would want to follow him?

David peeked up from the stairwell that led to the school basement, listening to the sound of Connor's retreating footsteps.

Phew! That was close!

He wasn't cut out to be a spy.

When he realized that Connor knew he was behind him, he'd run down the stairs hoping he wouldn't get caught.

He didn't know how much longer he could do this. Connor knew something was up and David did *not* want to get on his bad side.

Of course, there was Shawna's bad side to deal with as well. Especially if he didn't find out the name of Connor's Secret Santa for her.

David gulped.

He didn't know which would be scarier.

A mad Connor or a mad Shawna.

Even though he was getting a date with Shawna, David couldn't wait until tomorrow night's dance. All this spying would be over with and he could go back to his quiet, nerdy life.

After lunch, Noelle and Lily headed for their lockers. As they were leaving the cafeteria, they once again ran into Jason and Sonia, only this time they weren't all over each other, hugging and kissing and touching. This time they were arguing.

"I don't like the Secret Santa gifts you've been getting!" Jason exclaimed. "They're a little too romantic."

Sonia tossed her head. "Stop being so jealous!"

"I'm not jealous!"

"Yes, you are! And I'm sick of it! Can I help it if other guys are attracted to me?"

"No, but you don't have to show them you like it! What if one of them decided to ask you out?"

Sonia gave Jason a sly smile. "What's wrong with that?"

"You already have a boyfriend!" Jason sputtered. "Me!"

"You never said we were exclusive," Sonia shot back as they moved down the hallway, continuing to argue.

"Wow, this is better than an episode of *Laguna Beach*!" Noelle exclaimed.

"Maybe Jason might be getting a broken heart this Christmas," Lily laughed. "Serves him right!"

"Speaking of Secret Santas, did yours leave you anything today?" Noelle asked.

"A scented heart-shaped candle. It smells like peach," Lily said, opening her locker as Noelle did the same. "Hey, something just fell out of your locker." Lily bent down and picked up a small white envelope. "Oooh! Maybe it's a love note from your Secret Santa?"

Noelle eagerly snatched the envelope out of Lily's hand. "I wish!" She ripped open the note and read: *Sometimes what you're looking for is right under your nose. Meet me in the library at 3:00.*

"What does it say?" Lily asked impatiently, trying to read the note over Noelle's shoulder. "What does it say?"

"See for yourself." Noelle handed over the note with a smile. "It has to be from my Secret Santa! It has to be from Charlie!"

"Whoa! Slow down," Lily advised. "You still don't know for sure that Charlie is your Secret Santa."

"Hello! The balloons!" Noelle reminded Lily. "Party City. Do the math! He was giving me clues. How much more obvious does he need to be?"

"You're jumping to conclusions. Until he comes out and says, 'I'm your Secret Santa!' you don't know if he is or isn't!"

Noelle sighed. "Why must you be Miss Scrooge?" She snatched the note out of Lily's hand and waved it in her face. "I'm telling you this note is from Charlie and I'm going to be proved right at three o'clock this afternoon!"

At 3:45 Noelle was in the school library, still waiting to be proved right.

She checked the time on her watch for the umpteenth time, wondering where Charlie was.

Something unavoidable had to have happened and that's why he hadn't shown up. Otherwise he would have been there.

Unless Lily was right and he *wasn't* her Secret Santa.

No! Lily was wrong. Charlie *was* her Secret Santa. He had to be. It couldn't be anyone else.

Could it?

"Someone stand you up, Noelle?"

Mindy Yee slid into the seat next to Noelle. "You keep looking at your watch. Waiting for a guy? He must be something special. You've been here for forty-five minutes. That's forty-four minutes longer than I would ever wait."

Groan! Why hadn't she noticed Mindy was in the library? She'd probably been watching her every move. It was a good thing Charlie hadn't shown up, otherwise Mindy would have blabbed it to the entire school!

"My watch hasn't been working," Noelle said. "I need to get a new battery. That's all."

"Uh-huh," Mindy said skeptically. "Fine. Don't tell me. Keep your secret. But I think you were waiting for someone one. A guy. Simon Larson maybe?"

"Simon?" Noelle laughed. "Why would I be waiting for Simon?"

"I hear he and Amber are breaking up."

Noelle shrugged. "So?"

"I saw him watching you at lunch today!" Mindy announced.

So she had been right! But why was he watching her?

"There's nothing going on between Simon and me."

Mindy gave Noelle a knowing look. "But you'd like there to be, wouldn't you? Come on, you can tell me."

"Of course not! Simon and I have nothing in common!" Noelle decided to change the subject to something safer. "Get any gifts from your Secret Santa?"

"My gifts have been l-a-m-e!" Mindy moaned. "Today I got one of those stupid candy rings. You know, the ones that look like a big fat diamond? What am I supposed to do with it?"

Stick it in your big fat mouth so you can't gossip? Noelle wanted to say. Instead, she said, "Wear it?"

"I can't wait until this stupid Secret Santa exchange is over," Mindy grumbled. "Some loser definitely picked my name."

"Would love to chat some more, Mindy, but I've got to go," Noelle said, gathering up her books. She saw from the clock above the front desk that it was 4:00. The mystery of whoever left her the note would remain unsolved.

As Noelle was leaving the library, she ran into Celia, who gave her a warm smile.

"Hey, Noelle!"

"Hey, Celia." Noelle was surprised to see Celia by herself. With the exception of the Toys for Tots excursions, she was usually with Amber and Shawna. "What's going on?" She had to admit, Celia wasn't as bad as she thought she was. She was actually pretty nice. Of course, she *was* Charlie's Secret Santa. She couldn't forget that. "Are you excited about the Christmas dance tomorrow night?"

"I can't wait! Finally all this Secret Santa suspense will be over! I don't know about you, but it's driving me crazy."

"I can't wait to find out who my Secret Santa is," Noelle admitted. "He's been sooo romantic."

"I've been crushing on the guy whose name I picked," Celia confessed. "I hope he feels the same way about me."

"If I were you, I wouldn't get your hopes up too much," Noelle said gently. She didn't want to see Celia get hurt, but Charlie was hers first! "After all, the guy you're interested in could be involved with someone else. Or if he isn't, he might not feel the same way you feel about him."

"I think he's interested in me," Celia said confidently.

Celia's answer stunned Noelle. "You do? How?"

Before Celia could answer, Amber showed up at the end of the hallway. "Celia! What's keeping you? I want to get to the mall!"

Celia gave Noelle an embarrassed smile. "Sorry! Gotta go! I'll see you tomorrow!"

Noelle didn't want Celia to leave! She wanted to know why she thought Charlie was interested in her!

Simon was stuck in detention, falsely accused of a crime he hadn't committed!

He had been caught in the girls' locker room, but he hadn't been trying to take a peek at anyone! All he had been doing was leaving a Secret Santa gift for the girl whose name he'd picked. He'd been in the locker room just when all the girls were in the showers. Unfortunately, he'd been answering a call on his camera phone when Miss Ongstat, the girls' gym coach, had caught him and jumped to the wrong conclusion: Teenage Boy + Naked Girls + Camera Phone = Naked Photos. She hadn't believed his explanation, even when he'd shown her the gift he'd left behind. And his photo-less camera phone! Instead, he'd been given a detention slip for this afternoon.

He kept staring at the clock at the front of the classroom. Detention was for an hour and he wouldn't be a free man until 4:00. That was another fifteen minutes away.

This ruined all his plans!

He had left Noelle a note in her locker at lunchtime, asking her to meet him in the school library at 3:00. How long would she wait before giving up? He was jarred from his thoughts when he heard Miss Ongstat, today's detention teacher, shout, "What did I say about passing notes?" She jumped up from behind her desk and stormed toward Keesha Johnson and Dee Dee Howard, snatching up the note Keesha had just given to Dee Dee. "Just for that everyone is staying an extra fifteen minutes!"

Simon groaned. There was no way Noelle was going to still be waiting for him in the library. No way!

Finally, at 4:15, detention was over and Simon raced to the school library. Part of him was hoping Noelle would still be there, but she wasn't.

She was gone.

*   *   *

When Noelle got home from school, she found Ryan loading up the trunk of his car with wrapped presents for the Toys for Tots program.

"Need any help?" she asked, deciding to act like the fight they'd had the day before hadn't happened. It was on the tip of her tongue to ask if he knew where Charlie was but she didn't. She didn't want to start World War III! And she was sure everything was okay with Charlie. If it wasn't, Ryan would have said something

Ryan shrugged. "Sure. If you want. Thanks."

She knew that was Ryan's way of saying that he wasn't going to bring up their fight either.

As if reading her mind, Ryan said, "Charlie was supposed to help me, but he had a surprise dress rehearsal for the Christmas play."

Ah! That explained why he was a no-show at the library.

Noelle headed inside the Grant house where she found a pile of wrapped presents in the entry-way. She loaded up her arms and headed back outside. It took six trips, but finally the trunk and backseat of the car were filled with all the presents.

"I have to drop these off at the post office,"

Ryan said, slamming down the lid of the trunk. "Want to come along?"

"Sure. On the way back, can you drop me off at the mall? I have to pick up my dress for tomorrow night's dance."

Ryan held open the passenger door of the car. "Hop in. Your ride awaits!"

Chapter Seventeen

It was time for Shawna to pay up.

She and David were going out on their date.

There was no avoiding it. David had called her that morning and said that if she expected him to check out the girls who had left Connor gifts then they would be going out *today*.

If there was one thing Shawna hated, it was being told what to do. Even if she had planned on doing something, if someone *told* her to do it, she wouldn't! That's just the way she was.

But in this instance, she knew she had no choice.

Still, that didn't mean David would be calling *all* the shots.

She agreed to the date but told him the what/where/when of it.

She had decided they would see a movie at the mall and would meet at the theater. She lied to Amber and told her she wouldn't be around after school because she had an appointment at the dentist. To make sure no one recognized her, she disguised herself as best as she could. She hid her hair under a ski cap, wore a full-length down jacket with snow boots — thus making herself look shapeless — wrapped a scarf around the lower part of her face, and topped it all off with her huge Nicole Ritchie sunglasses.

She was completely unrecognizable. If she ran into anyone she knew, they wouldn't look twice because she didn't look anything like herself.

And that was the point.

Nothing against David, but girls like her did *not* go out with guys like him.

Besides, Connor was the only guy she wanted to date. And she certainly didn't want him to think she was cheating on him! Even with David!

When she got to the mall, she found David waiting outside the movie theater. There was no mistaking him. His jeans were too short and baggy, the back of his shirt was sticking out from beneath his jacket, and his hair was a mess, sticking out all over his head.

She sighed. Didn't nerds look into the mirror before going outside? Why didn't any of them have a sense of fashion?

He was screaming for a makeover!

She stopped in front of David and he stared at her blankly. Then she lowered her sunglasses down her nose. "It's me," she said.

At the sound of her voice, his entire face lit up. "You came!"

"Did you think I wouldn't?"

"I wasn't sure," he admitted.

"I always keep my word," Shawna said. "I hope you do the same thing."

"Of course I do!"

"Good. Then before we buy our tickets, you'll tell me what you found out about those girls from last night."

"None of them are Connor's Secret Santa."

"None of them?" Shawna asked, dejected. "Are you sure? Completely sure? Because Connor's Secret Santa left him a gift this morning. It was waiting in his first class." Luckily, Connor hated horror movies and had given the movie pass his Secret Santa had bought him to Simon. Who was this girl who kept buying such lousy gifts? Her not knowing what to buy Connor should make her feel a little bit better, but it didn't.

"I have some friends helping me out. Each one of us has been following a specific girl. They did leave gifts today, but they were for other guys. None of them left a gift for Connor."

Shawna sighed. "That means we're back at square one."

"Is it okay for me to buy the tickets?"

"Yes," Shawna said distractedly, trying to figure out what her next move should be. The Christmas dance was tomorrow night. She had to find a way to neutralize Connor's Secret Santa, otherwise she could lose him! Even if her gifts were lousy, who's to say she and Connor wouldn't hit it off? She needed to know who she was dealing with.

"I've got the tickets," David said, handing one to Shawna.

"Okay, here are the ground rules," Shawna said as they walked into the theater. "Are you listening because I'm only going to say them once."

"Should I be taking notes?" David asked,

patting down the pockets of his coat in search of a pen.

"You'll be able to remember them," Shawna said. "*Or else.*"

David gulped.

"There will be *no* hand-holding," Shawna began. "*No* arms around the shoulders and *no* rubbing of legs against each other. And absolutely, positively NO kissing!"

"How about sharing popcorn?" David asked meekly.

Shawna thought about the question, then nodded. "Sharing popcorn is allowed but *only* if the popcorn is unbuttered." She shuddered. "I hate that artificial gunk they squirt all over it."

"Me too!" David exclaimed. "Is there anything else you like munching on when you're watching a movie?"

"Well, I do like gummi bears," Shawna admitted. "And Raisinettes."

"Anything to drink?

"It would be nice to wash it all down with a diet Pepsi." Shawna reached into her shoulder bag to give David some money, but he waved it away.

"Put your money away. It's my treat."

Shawna was touched by David's generosity. She'd been on plenty of dates where the guy had expected her to pay for half of everything. Needless to say, there had been no second dates with those losers!

"That's awfully nice of you, David. Thanks."

"Anytime."

"If that's a hint for another date, the answer is no," Shawna quickly stated. She wasn't trying to be mean, but she didn't want David getting his hopes up. Today's date was a one-time and one-time-only thing.

"So what are we seeing?" she asked after David had gotten their snacks and they walked into the theater. She hadn't been paying attention when he bought the tickets. Her mind had been elsewhere.

"*Queen of the Fairies*," David said as they sat in their seats.

"A fantasy movie?" Shawna made a face, remembering the movie poster out in the lobby. It had shown a pink fairy riding on top of a blue unicorn. "Yuck!"

"You're going to love it. Trust me. It's very romantic."

Shawna noted David's use of the word *romantic*. She didn't want him getting any ideas. "Remember the ground rules," she reminded him, unbuttoning her coat.

"Am I allowed to breathe the same air as you?" David grumbled as the lights began to dim.

"Yes," Shawna whispered, reaching into the bag of popcorn he was holding. "And we can even share the same popcorn!"

Much to her surprise, Shawna enjoyed the movie. Granted, it was kind of weird, with fairies and elves and all sorts of creatures she'd never imagined existing, but David had been right. The story was very romantic. But it ended with a cliffhanger ending. Did that mean she would have to wait until the sequel before finding out what happened next? She asked David that question as they were leaving the movie theater.

"You don't have to wait until next year's sequel," David said as they walked out into the crowded mall, zigzagging their way around holiday shoppers. "You can buy the book."

"There's a book?"

"It's a seven-book series. Come on," he said, taking her hand and leading her into a bookstore. "I'll show you."

When they left the bookstore, Shawna had a shopping bag filled with the next six volumes of the series. David had told her that as soon as she finished the second book, she was going to want to read the third and the fourth and then all the rest. She very rarely bought novels, but if each book in the series ended the way the first one had, she couldn't be left hanging!

"We can talk about them after you finish reading them," David said.

"That may take a while," she admitted. "When it comes to books, I'm a slow reader. I'm much faster when it comes to magazines like *Vogue* and *US Weekly*."

"Trust me, once you start reading them, you'll be speeding through them."

"I suppose I could start with a chapter before I go to sleep at night and see what happens. I'll keep you posted." Shawna and David had reached the escalators for the first floor. "Thanks for the movie. It was fun." And it had been. David hadn't been all gropey the way she had expected him to be. The date had actually been nice. Of course, it wasn't a *real* date, but she hadn't suffered through it the way she'd been expecting.

"Is it okay if I walk you home?" David blurted out. "Most dates end that way, you know?"

Shawna decided to be nice. After all, it was the Christmas season. "Yes, you can walk me home." She held up a finger. "But there will be no kissing at the front door!"

"Who said anything about kissing?" David innocently asked as they stepped onto the escalator.

"I've been on plenty of dates. I know how guys think. They always want a kiss when they walk you home."

"You gave me the ground rules at the movie theater," David said. "I didn't forget."

"Okay."

When they reached the first floor, they began walking past a number of shops. As they passed a boutique, Shawna pointed at a dress in the window. It was midnight blue, shot with strands of silver, with spaghetti straps.

"That's what I'm going to wear to the dance tomorrow night," she told David. "The store asked if they could leave it in the window until I pick it up tomorrow. It's one of a kind. What do you think?"

Shawna didn't know why she was asking David for his opinion. Maybe it was because he was a guy and she wanted a guy's opinion. She wanted to look gorgeous tomorrow night — so gorgeous that Connor would do a double take and not want to break up with her. Because that's the feeling she was getting. Connor was going to break up with her at the dance tomorrow night. Why else would he be making himself so scarce these last few weeks?

"It's nice," David said, his tone of voice flat. Shawna instantly panicked.

"Nice? Just nice?" She wanted to grab him and shake him and have him tell her what was wrong with the dress. "That's all you have to say?"

"Well, if you want my honest opinion . . ." David began.

"Yes, I do! Honesty, please! You don't know how important tomorrow night is to me!"

"It's a nice dress, but why go with something so dark? Why not a lighter color?"

At first Shawna wanted to dismiss David's

opinion. But then she realized that what he said made sense. Perfect sense.

"How do you know about how a girl should dress?" she asked.

He shrugged. "I've been looking at girls for years. After a while you start to pick up a few things."

"You mean *drooling* over girls for years," Shawna teased.

"That too." David gazed at the dress in the window. "So are you still going to wear that?"

Shawna shook her head. "No. I actually have a different dress like the one you've described. I was going to wear it to my cousin Andrea's wedding next month, but I could wear it for the dance instead. I need to really wow Connor tomorrow night."

"You care about him, don't you?"

Until David said the words, Shawna didn't realize how true they were. "Yes, I do."

"Then why don't you tell him?"

Shawna shook her head. "I can't. What if he tells me he doesn't feel the same way?" She could never allow herself to be so vulnerable!

"But what if he does? What if *he* feels the same way *you* do, and *he's* afraid to tell you how he's feeling because he thinks *you* don't care about him."

"Then he should tell me!" Shawna exclaimed. "Don't you think?"

"But you're not telling him! It works the same way! Somebody's got to take the first step."

"Well it's not going to be me!" Shawna tore her eyes away from the dress in the window and decided to change the subject. She didn't want to talk about Connor anymore. "So what are you wearing tomorrow night?"

"Probably a suit."

"Not that gray pin-striped monstrosity that you wore last year for the Freshman Awards ceremony?" Shawna gasped. "With the black shirt and black tie?"

"Yes. Why? What's wrong with it?"

"It's five years out of style and you look like a gangster in it, that's what's wrong with it!"

Shawna grabbed David by the arm and pulled him into Abercrombie & Fitch. "Do you have an emergency credit card?"

"Yes."

"Good! Because we're going to do some serious shopping!"

Thirty minutes later Shawna had decked

David out in a pair of khakis, a white shirt, a red-and-blue striped tie, and a navy blue jacket with gold buttons. After they left the clothing store, they stopped into a drugstore, where Shawna handed David a container of hair gel.

"After you get out of the shower, just put a dab of this in the palm of your hand," she explained, "rub your hands together, and then run your fingers through your hair."

"What's that going to do?"

"It will give you a spiky look, but it will look much more preppy than your current stuck-your-finger-in-an-electrical-socket look."

David gasped at the price of the hair gel. "Fifteen bucks?!"

"It costs money to look good," Shawna said as she plucked David's emergency credit card out of his hand and gave it to the cashier.

After leaving the drugstore, they stopped at the men's fragrance department in Macy's where Shawna suggested David spritz himself with a few colognes. "See which scent you like best."

David began grabbing bottles, spraying himself everywhere.

"No! No! No!" Shawna cried, horrified. "I said spritz, not take a bath in!" She snatched a bottle of Ralph Lauren's Polo out of his hand. "Like this." She aimed the bottle at his wrist and pressed down lightly on its top. "Let it dry for a few seconds and then take a sniff." David did as he was instructed. "See? Doesn't that smell nice?"

"I like it," David said. "Let's buy it."

"It's going to cost way more than hair gel," Shawna warned.

"How much more?"

Shawna showed him the price.

"Yikes!"

"You don't have to buy it," Shawna said, putting the bottle down. "But a lot of girls like guys who smell good."

David plopped his emergency credit card down on the counter.

"It also comes in scented soap!" Shawna added.

After leaving Macy's with the cologne and soap, they went back out into the mall. As they were passing BRING THE BLING, a jewelry store, Shawna decided to pop in. She and Amber shopped in it all the time, and she still had to buy

Christmas presents for her sisters. Maybe she could find something inside.

The first thing she saw was a display of earrings. The designs were wild and funky and she decided to buy a pair for Chloe. Her younger sister was a little too straitlaced. She needed to loosen up! For Cassidy, she founded a colorful beaded necklace.

After she paid for her purchases and the store clerk handed her a shopping bag, she took a closer look at Shawna. "You're friends with Amber Davenport, right?"

"Uh-huh."

"Is she liking the bracelet she bought?"

"What bracelet?" Shawna didn't recall Amber recently buying a bracelet.

"The one made of glass beads," the clerk said.

Shawna wasn't sure she had heard the clerk correctly. "Glass beads?" The only glass-bead bracelet that Amber owned was the one her Secret Santa had given her.

Unless . . .

The clerk pointed to a display of beaded-glass bracelets . . . bracelets that were *identical* to the one owned by Amber.

"She bought it on Monday," the clerk said.

"In fact, she forgot her credit card receipt." She handed it to Shawna "Would you mind giving it to her?"

Shawna stared at the receipt with Monday's date on it.

Amber's Secret Santa had given her the bracelet on Tuesday.

Or so Shawna had thought!

Instantly, all the pieces fell into place.

Amber's Secret Santa hadn't bought her the bracelet.

Amber had bought it for herself!

Which meant she had probably bought *all* her Secret Santa gifts.

"Why do you look so mad?" David asked as they left the jewelry store.

"I'm not mad," Shawna lied, although she was. The entire week, Amber had rubbed her nose in the fact that her Secret Santa had bought her such expensive gifts, when all along she had been buying them. And then she had laughed at the sweet gifts left by Shawna's Secret Santa! Yesterday afternoon her Secret Santa had left another lollipop at her locker, and this morning she had found a gift certificate for an ice-cream cone at Ben & Jerry's.

For most of the walk home, Shawna was silent while David kept jabbering away. She wasn't paying any attention to him. All she could think about was Amber. She didn't know what she was going to do with the information she had found out, but she planned on doing something!

"Here we are," David said, once they reached her front yard.

It had started getting dark and some houses already had Christmas lights on. In her front yard, Chloe and Cassidy had made a snowman, using rocks for his eyes and mouth and a carrot stick for his nose.

"Thanks again for the movie," she said.

David held up his shopping bags. "Thanks for taking me shopping. Maybe you'll save me a dance tomorrow night?"

"Since you can't get a kiss, you'll settle for a dance?"

"You can't blame a guy for trying."

"*One* dance," Shawna said. "And only after Connor dances with me first. That is, *if* he even dances with me."

"I bet he does. In the meantime, I'll still keep an eye on him. See if his Secret Santa leaves him any more gifts."

"You don't have to do that."

"I know I don't, but I want to. And you don't have to go on another date with me. Consider this a freebie."

Just then Chloe came walking up the street, loaded down with her own shopping bags. "Guess everyone's doing last-minute shopping," she said. She turned to David. "Are you staying for dinner again?"

"I was just leaving," David said. "See you tomorrow, Shawna."

"Bye," she said as he started walking away.

"Are you sure you're not replacing Connor with him? You've been hanging out with him a lot lately."

"I'm not replacing Connor!" Shawna snapped, hating when Chloe butted into her personal business. "David's just a friend."

Chloe held up her hands in surrender. "Touchy, touchy."

As Shawna followed Chloe inside, her thoughts returned to Amber. For now she wasn't going to let Amber know she knew her secret, but at some point she was going to let her know she knew it.

She couldn't wait to see the expression on Amber's face when that happened!

Chapter Eighteen

House of Fashion was a zoo. Noelle couldn't believe there were so many girls still searching for a dress for the dance. She saw so many familiar faces from school. Luckily she had found her dress earlier in the week, and it had needed only a few alterations. Now it was ready to be picked up.

Ryan had dropped her off at the mall after they'd delivered the presents for the Toys for Tots program. They hadn't talked much. Instead, they'd listened to the radio and talked about Christmas specials, like *A Charlie Brown Christmas*, *Rudolph the Red-Nosed Reindeer*, *The Year Without a Santa Claus*, and their all-time favorite, *A Christmas Story*. Ryan had offered to wait around for her, but she still had some last-minute Christmas shopping to do and told him she'd get home with the bus.

Noelle was in the dressing room of House of Fashion, trying on her dress one last time. It was a plum satin slip-dress with spaghetti straps. Admiring herself in a full-length mirror, she loved the way it clung to her curves. She felt the dress made her look older. More mature. Like someone Charlie would want to go out with!

She still hadn't figured out what she was going to do with her hair. Or what kind of jewelry she was going to wear. She and Lily needed to discuss that tonight.

She was taking one final look at herself in the mirror when Celia and Amber walked into the dressing room. Noelle tried to see if Celia was carrying a dress, but she wasn't. Amber, on the other hand, did have a dress, and slipped into a changing stall. Seconds later she came out and made a face at her image.

"Blech! This dress is ugly! What was I even thinking trying something off-the-rack?"

"It doesn't look that bad," Celia said. "What do you think, Noelle?"

"I think it looks nice," Noelle said. And she

did. Amber had a gorgeous figure. She could wear a potato sack and make it look like a designer original.

"Nice isn't good enough!" Amber snapped. "I have to wow Charlie Grant tomorrow night!" After taking one last look at herself in the mirror, Amber flounced back into her changing stall.

"What did Amber mean by her comment?" Noelle asked.

Celia made sure no one was around, then whispered in Noelle's ear, "Amber is Charlie's Secret Santa."

Noelle's mouth dropped open. "But that's impossible! *You're* Charlie's Secret Santa."

Celia gave Noelle a confused look. "No, I'm not. Why would you say that?"

"Because I heard Amber say you were Charlie's Secret Santa," Noelle explained, her mind scrambling over what she'd just been told. It couldn't be. It just couldn't be! "It was right outside the cafeteria on Monday."

The confusion faded away from Celia's face. "Oh! Now I understand." Celia quickly filled Noelle in on Amber's scheme of pulling out the names of three seniors ahead of time. "That's why Amber is Charlie's Secret Santa. But don't tell her I told you! She'd kill me!"

Amber stormed out of her changing stall with her dress hanging lopsided off a hanger. "Come on, Celia. Let's head back to my house. I guess I'll have to pick one of the dresses my mother brought from Manhattan." She pulled out her cell phone as she walked back out into the store. "Maybe Shawna's back from the dentist and can help us out."

Noelle watched them disappear, her head spinning. Amber being Charlie's Secret Santa changed everything. Everything! She could handle Celia. She had a chance of outshining Celia "Beach Girl" Armstrong because of her shared history with Charlie. That gave her a tiny bit of an advantage. But *Amber*? *Amber Davenport?!* The girl was a she-wolf. A barracuda! A black widow spider. From as far back as seventh grade, she'd always gotten every guy she'd ever wanted and then moved on to the one she wanted after that! If she wanted Charlie to be her next boyfriend then Noelle didn't stand a chance.

What was she going to do?

★ ★ ★

Connor hated Christmas shopping. He always left it to the last minute. And because he did, he always had to do battle with holiday shoppers.

Luckily, he was almost finished. He just had to buy a gift for his mother and a gift for his father and then he could go home.

Oh, and then there was his final Secret Santa gift to pick up.

He had to admit, at first he thought the whole Secret Santa thing was dumb. But it was fun buying presents and leaving them to be found. Of course, his Secret Santa didn't have a clue what to buy him, but it was the thought that counted. He'd have to remember that tomorrow night when he met his Secret Santa.

Deciding to pop into The Gap, he found a hooded sweatshirt for his father. He was waiting in line to pay for it, staring out in the mall through the store's window, when he did a double take.

No, it couldn't be.

Could it?

He thought he saw Shawna walking through the mall with a nerdy redheaded guy, but it couldn't be her. Shawna would never be seen walking around in the outfit he had seen. And secondly, she'd never hang out with a nerd.

Or would she?

Was that why she'd been so distant lately?

He knew Amber and Simon were on the verge of breaking up.

And whenever Amber did something, Shawna did the same thing.

Was Shawna getting ready to break up with him?

Had she found herself a new boyfriend?

He left his spot in line and stuck his head out in the mall, searching the crowds for Shawna, but he couldn't find her. He went back in line, but he couldn't forget the question he'd asked himself.

Had Shawna found herself a new boyfriend?

If she had, there was only way to find out.

Tomorrow night at the Christmas dance.

The last thing Celia wanted to do was shop. But Amber was on a mission. She had to make sure she had the *perfect* outfit for tomorrow night's dance. After leaving House of Fashion, they had stopped in a shoe store and now Amber was trying on a variety of styles. Celia thought it was a little pointless, since Amber still didn't know what dress she would be wearing, but she didn't say anything. The only opinion that mattered was Amber's.

After trying on ten pairs of shoes, Amber finally decided to buy three pairs. As she was waiting in line to pay for them, Celia headed back out into the mall. Even though it was the Christmas season, when everything was supposed to be happy and jolly, all she wanted to do was go home and cry. She had been so sure Jake was her Secret Santa. So sure he was going to reveal himself as her Secret Santa at the dance when she was going to tell him that she had been crushing on him for months. So sure that they were then going to kiss and start dating and become a couple. She had built up an elaborate fantasy in her mind, and now it was gone.

"What's with the long face?"

Celia whirled around and saw Freddy standing behind her.

"Is everything okay?" he asked. "You seem upset."

Celia could see the concern on Freddy's face and it touched her. He thought something was really wrong. How could she tell him the truth? He'd think she was an airhead!

"It's nothing," Celia said. "Just something silly."

"It can't be too silly if it has you looking so sad." Freddy took Celia by the hand and walked her over to one of the wooden benches scattered throughout the mall. "Anything you want to talk about?" he asked as they sat down. "I'm a good listener."

Before she could stop herself, Celia blurted it out. "Jake's not my Secret Santa, and I was so sure it was him!"

"How do you know it's not Jake?"

"He was out sick today! That means he couldn't have left me the daisies this morning. And if he didn't leave me the daisies, then he didn't leave me any of my other gifts."

"That's what's gotten you so upset?"

Celia buried her face in the palm of her hands. "I know, I know. It's stupid, isn't it?"

Freddy slowly pulled Celia's hands away from her face. "No, it isn't," he said. "Okay, so Jake isn't your Secret Santa. That doesn't mean you can't tell him that you have feelings for him. That you like him. Who knows? Maybe he might have feelings for you. Did you ever stop to think of that?"

Celia shook her head. "I didn't."

"It's Christmas!" Freddy exclaimed. "Anything is possible."

"There you are!" Amber exclaimed as she hurried over with three shopping bags. "I didn't know where you had disappeared to. Come on! I want to stop in the MAC store before we leave. I need to buy a new lipstick and mascara."

"Don't forget what I said," Freddy whispered as he walked away.

After Freddy left, Celia mulled over his words. He was right. Just because Jake wasn't her Secret Santa, that was no reason not to tell him how she felt. After all, she'd been crushing on him for months. She was going to have to do something about it eventually. Why not tomorrow night at the Christmas dance?

As Celia was leaving the mall with Amber, she caught sight of Freddy in a card store. He was waiting in line with a roll of silver foil wrapping paper decorated with white snowflakes.

He was such a nice guy, she realized. Always there. Always willing to listen. She was really lucky to have him as a friend.

She hoped he got exactly what he wanted this Christmas.

He deserved it.

Froggy was a man on a mission.

After talking with Celia, he had come up with a plan.

A plan that would give her exactly what she wanted this Christmas.

He rang the doorbell of Jake's house and waited for it to be answered. Seconds later, the door was opened by a sniffling Jake, who was wearing a pair of flannel pajama bottoms and a Scissor Sisters T-shirt.

"How are you feeling?" Froggy asked, stepping inside out of the cold.

"Just one of those twenty-four-hour bugs." Jake blew his nose into a tissue. "What are you doing here? Did Gloria send you to check on me? Does she not believe I'm sick?"

"Gloria didn't send me," Froggy explained. "I'm here because I want to ask you to do something for me."

"What?" Jake asked as they headed up to his bedroom.

Froggy took a deep breath and then said the words before he chickened out. "I want you to be Celia's Secret Santa."

Jake did a double take. "You want *me* to be Celia's Secret Santa? Why? You're her Secret Santa."

"Celia has a crush on you," Froggy explained, taking off his coat and tossing it on Jake's bed. The room was a mess, with stacks of unfolded clothes all over the floor, piles of CDs and DVDs, and a stack of empty pizza boxes. "She has for months."

"Really? Huh." Jake seemed thrown for a loop. "I didn't know that."

"Until today, she thought you were the one leaving her all those gifts."

"What happened today?" Jake asked.

"I left her some flowers, and she thought they were from you until she found out you were out sick."

"Oops!"

"Oops is right! But it's nothing that can't be fixed. So, will you do it? Will you be Celia's Secret Santa and pretend you've been the one sending her gifts?"

"But I haven't. Besides, what's the point? You're the one who has feelings for Celia, not me."

"I know," Froggy admitted. "But all I want is for Celia to be happy and what will make her happy is you. You have to admit, she's pretty special."

"She is kinda cool," Jake said. "But I don't feel about her the way you do."

"That's because you don't know her," Froggy argued. "You've never thought of her romantically, have you? But what if you did? You'd go out with a girl like Celia, wouldn't you?"

"Maybe," Jake slowly answered.

"Please, Jake," Froggy begged. "Do this for me?"

"We already settled things up, remember? I was going to find stuff out about her so you could buy Secret Santa presents."

"Consider it an early Christmas present."

"Who says I was buying you a present?"

"I bought you one. Please, Jake? I promise I'll never ask you for anything ever again."

Jake sighed, running his fingers through his long hair. "Okay, okay, I'll do it, but I can't promise that this is going to lead to anything. I'll tell her I'm her Secret Santa and I'll take her out on a date, but if there are no sparks between us, that's it." Jake shook his head.

"You must really care about Celia to give her up this way."

"I do," Froggy said, trying not to imagine Celia and Jake dancing together at the Christmas dance tomorrow night. It hurt too much. He wanted to be the one holding her close. He wanted to be the one whispering in her ear. He wanted to be the one to kiss her good night. But when you cared about someone, you made sacrifices. You put their happiness first. "I really do."

"What am I going to do?" Noelle wailed into her cell phone, pacing from one end of her bedroom to the other. "What am I going to do?"

"Noelle, calm down," Lily advised. "Getting upset isn't going to accomplish anything."

"How can I not get upset? Amber is Charlie's Secret Santa."

"Only through underhanded means! I'm sure if we told Principal Hicks what Amber had done, she'd be in major hot water."

"That isn't going to accomplish anything. It will only get Celia into trouble with Amber. Plus, when Charlie finds out what Amber did so she could get his name, I bet he'll be flattered!"

"Good point. I hadn't thought of that. Never underestimate a guy's ego."

"Or his reaction to a hot babe!" Noelle moaned, running her fingers through her hair. "Amber's going to be all va-va-va-vooming tomorrow night, and Charlie's tongue is going to roll out of his mouth like a cartoon character's! She's hot, I'm not! I don't stand a chance!"

"Let me give this some thought," Lily said. "I'm sure I can come up with some sort of plan to eliminate Amber."

"What kind of plan?" Noelle asked, trying not to get her hopes up.

"I don't know. Yet. But I'm sure I'll come up with something."

"Hurry!" Noelle exclaimed. "We don't have much time. The dance is in less than twenty-four hours!"

Chapter Nineteen

Noelle woke up before her alarm clock went off and jumped out of bed. She hadn't been able to sleep a wink the night before. Either she was tossing and turning, unable to get comfortable no matter how many times she fluffed her pillow, or she was having nightmares — nightmares featuring Amber as Mrs. Charlie Grant! — that kept jolting her awake. But now it was morning and the day she had been waiting for had finally arrived.

Tonight was the Christmas dance!

In twelve hours she was finally going to be able to tell Charlie how she felt about him.

There was just one little problem.

Amber.

Luckily, Lily had come up with a solution.

Okay, it wasn't a *nice* solution, and Charlie was the one who was going to suffer — although not for very long! — but it was the only thing Lily had been able to come up with on such short notice.

The solution was simple: a blue-and-white scarf dusted with cat hair (courtesy of Lily's tabby, Miss Kitty).

Originally, the scarf — without the cat hair — was going to be Noelle's last Christmas gift to Charlie, along with a note that said: *We'll get to meet tonight at the Christmas dance. Be sure to wear this so I'll be able to find you!*

The cat hair was added because Charlie was allergic to cats.

Once the scarf was wrapped around Charlie's neck, his eyes would water and he would start sneezing like crazy. Romance would be the last thing on his mind!

At first Noelle had been reluctant to leave the tainted scarf. It was so mean! But as Lily kept reminding her, she had no choice. Besides, all was fair in love and war, especially when dealing with Amber! They had seen Charlie in the past when his cat allergy kicked in. It wasn't a pretty picture. He became such a sneezing, watery mess, he came pretty close to being gross! There was no way Amber was going to want to hug/kiss/get close to something that wasn't hunkalicious!

After Lily had gone home last night, Noelle had sneaked over to the Grants' and left her present for Charlie on the front porch. With the exception of the twinkling Christmas lights, the entire house had been pitch-black.

She peeked out her bedroom window to see if her package was still on Charlie's front porch, but it wasn't.

Noelle gulped.

She hoped Charlie didn't decide to wear the scarf before tonight. If he did, her entire plan would be ruined!

After pulling her head back inside, she got dressed, deciding on a purple turtleneck, black jeans, and boots. After brushing her teeth and adding some mascara and lip gloss, she was ready to go.

As she hurried down the front stairs, her mother called out to her from the kitchen, telling her to eat something before she left for school. Wanting to keep her mother happy, she dashed into the kitchen and grabbed a banana. Then she gave her mother and father, who were both sipping their morning cups of coffee and munching on bagels smothered with cream cheese, a quick kiss on the cheek before hurrying back to the front hall and bundling herself up.

When she opened the front door, she found a present waiting for her. Her heart began pounding with excitement and butterflies fluttered in her stomach. Taking off her gloves, she quickly unwrapped the package and discovered a tiny gold key with a note: *Only you have the key to my heart. No one else. If I give you my heart, will you take a look at what's inside?*

Noelle made a fist around the key, holding it tight, almost as if she was afraid she would lose it. Then she gazed in the direction of Charlie's house and whispered, "Yes. Yes! I'll take a look at what's inside!"

When Noelle got to school, it was a madhouse. Everyone was buzzing with excitement not only because that night was the dance and Secret Santas would be revealed, but it was also the last day of classes. They would then be off for two whole weeks! No teachers. No schoolwork. No homework. Just two weeks of fun!

She was at her locker, hanging up her jacket and searching for her books for her morning classes, when Simon sidled up to her. She had noticed him heading in her direction from the corner of her eye, but hadn't thought anything of it. Until he was standing next to her. Like right in her personal space! Why was he standing *so* close? She moved a few inches back but he instantly closed the distance. *What* was his problem?!

"I know," he whispered into her ear.

"Know what?" Noelle asked, confused. What was he talking about?

Simon gave her a coy smile. "Who Connor's Secret Santa is."

Noelle gasped. "You're not going to tell, are you?" How had he found out? Lily had been so careful.

"Of course not!"

"Because that would ruin everything," Noelle said. "Everyone's supposed to find out tonight at the dance."

"Don't worry," Simon reassured her. "I know how to keep a secret."

"Good." Noelle expected Simon to leave, but he didn't. He just kept staring at her with an intense expression on his face. Why the sudden attention from him all of a sudden? It was freaking her out! "Is there anything else you want to tell me?" she asked, slamming her locker door shut.

"Those gifts were all wrong for Connor, you know that, don't you?"

"He wasn't easy to shop for," she admitted.

"But they were perfect for me." Simon leaned closer to Noelle. She could smell the scent of his cologne. It was different from what Charlie usually wore. She didn't like it. "Do you think Connor's Secret Santa might be willing to give me a dance tonight?"

Aha! That's why Simon was acting so strangely. He was interested in Lily! Things must definitely be over with him and Amber.

Noelle gave Simon a smile. "I think that might be possible. Very possible."

Simon smiled back. "Great! Then I'll see you tonight."

As soon as Simon disappeared down the hallway, Noelle raced to find Lily. When she finally found her on the way to the school library, she relayed her entire conversation with Simon. Lily's mouth dropped open as she listened to Noelle's words.

"Simon Larson wants to dance with me? *Me?* Are you sure?"

"He said he wanted a dance with Connor's Secret Santa. That's you, isn't it?"

"Yes, but I can't believe it!"

"Believe it! I don't know how he found out that you're Connor's Secret Santa, but he did!"

Lily gasped. "Do you think he could be *my* Secret Santa?"

Noelle shrugged. "Who knows? You won't have to wait much longer to find out. Why? What makes you think it could be him?"

Lily reached into her pocket and took out a key chain with half a heart dangling from it. "I found this from my Secret Santa this morning with a note."

"What did the note say?"

"That the other piece of the heart would get added at the dance tonight."

Noelle squealed with delight. "How super romantic! Mark my words, tonight is going to be a night that neither one of us forgets!"

All Shawna wanted to do was forget what she had found out the day before. But she couldn't.

Amber had lied to her. And it hurt! She and Amber were supposed to be best friends, but everything between them was always a competition. And that was because of Amber. Amber always had to be better than everyone else, especially Shawna. It didn't used to be that way. Where had her best friend gone?

That morning, Shawna managed to avoid Amber because they didn't have any classes together. The first time she saw her was at lunch, when she joined her at their table. Celia was also there, munching on some carrot sticks while paging through the latest issue of *People*.

"Where've you been?" Amber asked. "I've been leaving messages for you since yesterday afternoon."

"I've been busy."

"With what?"

"Christmas stuff."

"Speaking of Christmas, look at these!" Amber exclaimed, pointing to the dangling earrings she was wearing. "They're from my Secret Santa."

"Your Secret Santa gave those to you?" Shawna asked.

Amber nodded, twisting her head from side to

side. "Aren't they fab? I didn't think today's gift could top the perfume I got yesterday, but I was wrong!"

"Very pretty," Celia added. "But also very expensive! Those had to have cost more than what we're allowed to spend."

The words slipped out before Shawna could stop them. "Money's no object when you can charge it to Daddy's credit card, right, Amber?"

"What's that supposed to mean?" Amber asked.

"Nothing," Shawna said, backing off.

"Now that you're here we can talk about tonight," Amber said. "Celia, close that magazine!"

Celia instantly did as Amber requested.

"I figured we could all get ready for the dance at my house," Amber said. "Come over at seven and we can do our hair and makeup. Then the limousine I've rented can take us to the dance."

"You've rented a limo?" Celia asked. "Why? It's not like this is the prom or anything."

"I don't know how you did things out in California," Amber sniffed, "but out here, making an entrance is important. You're getting a free ride, so stop complaining!"

"She wasn't complaining," Shawna said, sticking up for Celia. "All she did was ask a question."

"When we get to the dance," Amber continued, ignoring Shawna, "and it's time for Secret Santas to be revealed, make sure you don't spend too much time with whoever's picked your name if they're not on our level."

"Our level?" Celia asked.

"She means if they're losers," Shawna explained.

"Exactly!" Amber exclaimed.

"You don't really believe that, do you?" Celia asked, her voice filled with shock. "If someone's been nice enough to buy me gifts all week, I'm going to thank them. And I'm going to get to know them. Isn't that the whole point of the holiday season?"

"Spare me the Cindy Lou Who speech," Amber said, rolling her eyes.

Celia rose from the table and gathered her books. "Not a problem."

Amber's eyes narrowed and Shawna could see her temper start to rise. She had to do something fast, otherwise Celia was going to get ripped into by Amber. It was time to turn the tables.

"So how much time are you going to give yourself tonight?" Shawna asked Amber.

"What are you talking about?"

Shawna reached into her pocket and handed Amber the receipt the clerk from the jewelry store had given her the night before. "You forgot this the other day when you bought your bracelet. You know, the one made of glass beads. The one your Secret Santa gave you."

"You were sending gifts to yourself?" Celia gasped.

"What? What? Who was sending gifts to themselves?" Mindy Yee gasped just as she was walking by with her lunch tray. Her eyes darted from Amber to Shawna to Celia. She could sense the tension in the air and plopped herself down in a chair. "What's going on?"

"No, I wasn't," Amber said, ignoring Mindy's question. "I liked the bracelet so much, I bought another one just like it."

"How did you know where they were being sold?" Shawna asked. "And you bought the bracelet the day *before* your so-called Secret Santa left it for you. Check the date on the receipt."

"Receipts don't lie," Mindy said, trying to take a peek at the receipt Amber was holding.

"Why would you lie about your Secret Santa?" Celia asked.

"Amber always has to be better than everyone else. Even when it comes to Christmas," Shawna said.

Mindy rubbed one finger on top of another, red lips pursed. "Shame, shame."

"That's so sad," Celia said.

Hearing Celia's words, Amber's face turned red with rage. "I don't have to explain anything to any of you!" she shouted, crumpling the receipt in her hand.

"That's right, you don't," Shawna said, leaving the table. She had a feeling her friendship with Amber was over.

But it had been over for a long time already.

She just hadn't wanted to admit it to herself.

Celia hurried after Shawna. She couldn't believe what she had just witnessed. It was better than a daytime soap opera!

It also meant she was free!

She couldn't imagine Amber still wanting to be friends with her. Not when she knew Amber had been sending Secret Santa gifts to herself!

300

She'd be too embarrassed and Mindy was sure to spread the story throughout school. When Celia had left the table, Mindy had already pulled out her BlackBerry, fingers flying over the keys.

Celia tried to catch up with Shawna, wanting to get the full story, but the halls were jam-packed with students and she lost her in the crowd. Then the bell for next period rang and she had to hurry to Anatomy and Physiology. She'd just have to wait until after school to talk to Shawna.

When she arrived in the lab, she found Freddy already in his seat, his nose buried in a book like always. He looked up as she sat down next to him.

"Feeling any better than yesterday?" he asked, closing his book.

"Actually, I am," she said. "I've decided I'm going to take your advice and talk to Jake at the dance tonight."

"You are? How come?"

Celia shrugged. "Why not? What have I got to lose? I tell him I like him and either he says he likes me back or he doesn't."

Celia leaned over to Freddy and gave him a kiss on the cheek. She could see she'd taken him by surprise because he instantly blushed.

"Hey!" he exclaimed, placing a hand on his cheek. "What was that for?"

"Just my way of saying thank you."

Froggy didn't think he was ever going to wash his cheek again. Celia had kissed him. Okay, it wasn't an on-the-lips kiss, but it was still a kiss!

And she hadn't been grossed out.

She had wanted to kiss him!

Suddenly, Froggy was seized by doubts.

If Celia had wanted to kiss him on the cheek, who's to say she wouldn't kiss him on the lips?

Was he doing the right thing by stepping aside?

Or was he making a mistake?

Should he follow his own advice and tell Celia how he felt about her?

He glanced over and saw she had that same goofy smile on her face that she'd had earlier in the week. At the time, he had wondered who she was thinking about. Now he knew it had been Jake. And she was thinking of him again.

No, he couldn't undo things.

As much as his heart was breaking, as much

as he hated losing her, he couldn't tell her how he felt.

Celia had feelings for Jake.

Jake was the guy she wanted.

Not him.

Celia was totally surprised when she got to Art class.

Standing by her desk with a bouquet of purple daisies was Jake.

"These are for you," he said, handing the flowers to her.

"Why?" she asked.

"I wasn't sure if you got the bouquet I sent yesterday when I was out sick, so I wanted to make sure you got these."

Hearing those words, Celia almost dropped the bouquet. "What did you say?"

"I know we're supposed to wait until tonight to reveal ourselves," Jake said, "but I can't wait anymore. Celia, I'm your Secret Santa."

"B-b-but you can't be my Secret Santa," Celia sputtered. "You were out sick yesterday. I thought —"

Jake cut her off. "Even Secret Santas have elves who help them."

Jake was her Secret Santa. She had been right!

Jake moved in close to Celia and her heart began pounding with excitement. Was he going to kiss her?

"So I know this is short notice, but I was wondering if you would be my date for the dance tonight?"

Celia threw her arms around Jake's neck. She didn't even have to think about her answer. "I'd love to!"

Chapter Twenty

Noelle felt like a princess!

She admired herself in the full-length mirror behind her closed bedroom door, loving what she saw. From her hair to her makeup to her dress, everything was perfect!

To match her plum-colored dress, she was wearing plum satin slingbacks, and her hair was coiled on top of her head in a sexy chignon, jeweled hairpins added for a touch of elegance.

She'd gone light on her makeup, but used just enough to enhance her features: blush on her cheekbones, a smoky shade of violet eye shadow, a touch of mascara, and plum lipstick with an added touch of lip gloss for shimmer and shine.

But the finishing touch was the last gift she'd received from her Secret Santa. She had found it waiting on her front porch when she got home from school that afternoon. It was a wrist corsage of tiny pink roses and white roses. The note attached asked her to wear the corsage to the dance that night.

Of course she would!

She slipped the corsage on her wrist and took one last look at herself in the mirror, pleased with what she saw.

She was ready to go!

When she walked downstairs, her father instantly began taking pictures with his digital camera.

"You look beautiful," her mother gushed as Noelle slipped into a white wool overcoat that she wore only on special occasions. "Now, I know you're in a hurry to get to the dance, but could you do me a favor and drop this package off next door? The mailman left it here by mistake."

"Sure," Noelle said, taking the package. She saw it was addressed to Charlie's mother. Although she had hoped to make an entrance at the dance, maybe Charlie would still be home. Maybe he'd even give her a ride and they could walk in together as a couple! Wouldn't that piss off Amber! Although Amber had other things to be pissed off about. The entire school knew she had been sending Secret Santa gifts to herself. Everyone was talking about it. Or rather, laughing about it. Amber's reign of terror was over. Ding-dong the witch is dead!

She gave her parents a kiss good-bye, then hurried next door and rang the bell, waiting for it to be answered.

When the front door opened, she found herself staring at a very dapper and handsome Charlie. He was wearing a dark blue suit with an open-collar white shirt, his blond hair slicked back with gel. Very yummy!

Charlie whistled as he gazed at Noelle. "Wow! You look great. Who knew you cleaned up so nicely? Let's see what's under the coat."

Noelle blushed although she loved what she was hearing! Charlie hardly ever noticed what she was wearing or how she looked. Was it because he was going to reveal himself as her Secret Santa later that night?

"Thanks," she said shyly, unbuttoning her coat and letting him see her dress as she gave a quick whirl. Then she made a point of waving her wrist in front of his face. "Look what I found waiting for me this afternoon."

Charlie barely glanced at the corsage as he took the package Noelle handed him, placing it on a table in the hallway. "So, are you going to act all surprised tonight?"

"What do you mean?"

Charlie's eyes widened with surprise. "Don't tell me you haven't figured it out? I thought you would have by now."

"Figured what out?"

Charlie looked around, as if afraid of being overheard. "That Ryan is your Secret Santa."

WHAT?!

Noelle was floored. *Ryan* was her Secret Santa?!

All those *romantic* gifts had come from *Ryan*?!

"Ryan? Your brother Ryan?" Noelle croaked, barely able to get the words out, she was so shocked.

Charlie nodded. "You didn't have a clue, did you? I can tell from the expression on your face."

No, she did *not* have a clue. Ryan couldn't be her Secret Santa. Charlie was supposed to be her Secret Santa. Charlie. Not Ryan!!!

"Promise not to tell him I told you? He'd kill me for spilling the beans, but I knew you'd be excited."

"I won't tell," she said, her mind still reeling.

"You two are perfect for each other." Charlie glanced at the time on his watch. "Yikes! I gotta go! I'm late. Liz, my new girlfriend, is waiting for me to pick her up."

"Liz Carmichael, the head cheerleader?" Noelle asked, knowing there was only one Liz that mattered at North Ridge High. Just like there was only one Kristy, one Sherry, one Theresa, and one Dana who mattered. And all of them were Charlie's exes. Suddenly she felt like the biggest fool. She had never stood a chance with Charlie. He was never going to see her as anything more than the girl next door. Ryan had tried to warn her, but she wouldn't listen to him.

Charlie smiled. "Uh-huh! She's super hot! We just started going out last week. Who knows how long it's going to last, but for now it's fun!"

"And that's all that matters? Having fun?"

Charlie shrugged. "What else is there?"

How about caring about someone? Noelle wanted to scream. How about getting to know them? She couldn't believe she had been crushing on Charlie for so many years without seeing him as he really was! For him, going out with girls was like going through a box of Kleenex!

Why hadn't she known this about him? Well, if she was honest with herself, she had. Ryan had told her. But she hadn't wanted to believe him. She'd seen only what she wanted to see. She'd turned Charlie into perfect boyfriend material when he wasn't.

Ryan wasn't perfect.

But he was kind.

And thoughtful.

And he cared about her.

And she'd been too blind to see it.

Charlie then gave Noelle a kiss on the top of her head. Like a big brother would give his little sister before tucking her into bed! Suddenly, she became infuriated. She wanted to yell. She wanted to scream! But she couldn't do that. She could do something else, though.

"Don't forget your scarf," she said sweetly, reaching for the blue-and-white scarf that was draped over the banister behind Charlie, making a point of snugly wrapping it around his neck. "Don't want you catching a cold."

"Thanks!"

"My pleasure," Noelle said, watching him leave.

After Charlie left, Noelle headed for the dance,

still in shock, trying to make sense of what she'd learned.

Ryan had sent her all those gifts?

Ryan had been the one crushing on her all this time?

How could she have been so dumb? Suddenly it all made sense. His jealousy. His anger. His hurt. All she ever did was go on and on and on about Charlie and the entire time *Ryan* had feelings for *her*.

What was she going to do?

How was she going to make it up to him?

Could she make it up to him?

Or was it too late?

Chapter Twenty-One

As soon as the doorbell rang, Celia rushed to answer it.

She had been dressed and waiting for Jake for over an hour. Before opening the front door, she took one final peek at herself in the hallway mirror. She'd spent hours getting ready and wanted to make sure she looked perfect.

She was wearing an ivory cotton-lace mini-dress with bell-shaped sleeves and twill ribbon at the bust. Her shoes were ice-blue satin pumps. For her hair, she'd decided to pull it back and wear a pair of silver earrings that were long and dangling. Her makeup was very minimal — mascara to highlight her blue eyes and blush on her cheeks. The overall look was California beach girl with a touch of elegance.

When she opened the front door, she found Jake waiting with his hands behind his back. He was dressed in black jeans, black boots, and a black T-shirt, along with his black motorcycle jacket. His long hair was tied back and he wore a pair of black mirrored sunglasses.

Jake slid his sunglasses down his nose with one hand and gave Celia a smile. "Ready to do some dancing?"

"Only after you tell me what you're hiding behind your back," Celia said.

"One last gift from your Secret Santa," he said, handing her a package wrapped in silver foil with white snowflakes.

Celia instantly recognized the wrapping paper. She had seen Freddy buying it the day before at the mall.

She gasped.

Suddenly, all the pieces fell into place.

Why hadn't she figured it out sooner?

She stared at Jake. "You're not my Secret Santa, are you?"

Her question threw Jake for a loop. A moment of uncertainty washed over his face, and she could see he was scrambling to come up with an answer.

But she already had hers.

There was no longer a doubt in her mind.

"What do you mean?" He laughed. "Of course I am."

She could hear the nervousness in his voice. Celia shook her head. "No, you're not. It's Freddy, isn't it? Freddy is my Secret Santa."

It all made sense.

Why Freddy was always so shy around her.

It was because he liked her.

Why he had run off the other day after they'd fallen into the snowbank when they'd been throwing snowballs at each other.

It was because he'd wanted to kiss her, but he'd been afraid to.

Freddy had bought all her Secret Santa gifts, not Jake. He and Jake had been working together. Jake had been telling Freddy everything he found out about her and Freddy had been using the information. That was why he had been reading Jane Austen the other day! It gave him something to talk about with her.

Celia waved the wrapped package in his face. "Don't lie to me. I saw Freddy buying this wrapping paper last night."

Jake sighed. "You're right," he admitted.

"Freddy is your Secret Santa. He's crazy about you — he has been for months — but he didn't think you'd be interested. And when he heard that you had a crush on me, he asked me to pretend I was your Secret Santa even though I had picked Shawna Westin's sister, Chloe. He wanted to give you what you wanted this Christmas."

"But why would you do that?" Celia asked. "I don't understand. You don't care about me, do you?"

Jake sighed and looked around the porch. Then he looked back at Celia and reluctantly said, "No, I don't."

Ouch! Harsh! But Celia knew those were the words he was going to say. And surprisingly, they didn't hurt. Deep down, she had known Jake wasn't her Secret Santa. It just didn't add up — especially after she'd gotten those flowers when he'd been out sick. No high school guy was *that* romantic! — and she'd never gotten the sense that he was interested in her. But with Freddy, she'd always wondered why he acted the way he did when he was around her, but never given it much thought. She should have connected the dots sooner!

"Then why?" she asked again. "Why pretend?"

Jake shrugged. "Sometimes when a friend asks you to do something for them, you just do it. No questions asked."

"I was your Secret Santa," Celia said. "Surprise!"

Jake winced. "Guess I was a bit harsh on your presents."

Celia squeezed two fingers together. "Just a little bit. But your gifts —" Celia caught herself, "I mean, Freddy's gifts — were always perfect."

Jake took off his sunglasses and stared into Celia's eyes. "You're great, Celia. Really, you are. But I can't explain why I don't like you the way you like me. It's nothing personal. I like you as a friend, that's all. If we'd gone out a couple of times, who knows? Something might have developed. But why take a chance on something that might not happen when you have a sure thing? Right now you've got a guy who's crazy about you and that guy is Freddy."

Celia knew Jake was right.

Now she had to figure out what she was going to do about it.

★   ★   ★

Froggy was sitting on his couch, a bowl of buttered popcorn in his lap, the remote control by his side, getting ready for a *Heroes* marathon on the Sci-Fi Channel. He sighed. Could he be any nerdier? But what else did he have to do? Everyone else was at the school dance. Even David.

He tried not to think about the dance but he couldn't. His thoughts kept returning to Celia and Jake. Were they dancing together? Laughing together? Were they hugging? Kissing?

He had to stop torturing himself this way. He'd made his decision and he had to live with it.

He'd lost Celia.

She was with Jake now.

The opening credits on *Heroes* were just starting when the doorbell rang. His parents were out doing some last-minute Christmas shopping, so that meant he had to answer the door. He paused the TV — thank God for DVR! — and went to see who it was. When he opened the door, he was stunned to see Celia.

He was even more stunned when she threw her arms around him in a hug and gave him a kiss.

"W-w-what was that for?" he sputtered in shock.

"You are the sweetest guy I've ever known, and I'm so glad you're my Secret Santa."

"Y-y-you know?"

"Of course I know!" she exclaimed. "Did you think I wouldn't find out? Why didn't you tell me?"

Froggy shrugged, still unable to believe that Celia was here. Standing on his front porch. Talking to him. Kissing him! Not Jake. HIM!!! "I didn't know how." Froggy gestured at Celia with his hands. "You're you. Super gorgeous." He pointed to himself. "And I'm me. Super nerdy. We're like Beauty and the Beast."

"That's a horrible thing to say!"

"You know what I mean. Guys like me don't go out with girls like you. Besides, I thought you were interested in Jake."

"And that's why you stepped aside?" Celia asked.

Froggy blushed. "You told me you liked him."

"Yes, I did," Celia admitted. "But he doesn't like me."

"So am I the consolation prize?"

"No!" Celia shouted. "This entire week you made me think that Jake was my Secret Santa. That Jake was doing such sweet, wonderful things, but it was really you! *You* were the one I was falling for, only I didn't know it. And now I do." Celia stepped closer to Froggy, looking deep into his eyes. "No one has ever been that nice to me before. Did you stop to think that if you hadn't been pushing Jake in my direction, I might have realized you had feelings for me?" Then she jabbed a finger in Froggy's chest. "Or you could have just asked me out. I don't bite!"

"I was afraid to."

"Then I guess you need the girl to do the asking."

"Huh?"

Celia turned Froggy around and pushed him in the direction of the stairs. "Hurry up and change your clothes because we've got a dance to get to!"

Celia didn't have to tell him twice. Froggy raced upstairs to his bedroom, pulling off his sweatshirt and kicking off his sneakers. He didn't know how Celia had figured things out, but he didn't care. She had kissed him! And they were going to the dance together!

Who said Christmas wishes didn't come true?

Chapter Twenty-Two

The North Ridge High gym had been transformed into a winter wonderland.

Noelle couldn't believe the spectacular job the dance committee had done. Even though she was inside, it felt like she was outside. Everywhere she looked, it was snow white. There were huge snowflakes hanging from the ceiling, there was a maze of snow-covered Christmas trees decorated with shimmering silver balls and draped with twinkling white lights — almost like a hidden forest — at the back of the gym, rows of white streamers were hung across the ceiling, and teeny-tiny bits of white confetti danced in the air like falling snowflakes, blown by hidden fans.

A slow song was playing and couples were dancing closely.

As she walked through the gym, she saw some of her friends and waved distractedly at them, not stopping to talk. She couldn't. She was on a mission to find Ryan, and she wouldn't stop searching until she found him.

But what happened once she did find him?

She still didn't know what she was going to say to him. What could she say that would make up for all the years of ignoring him? Of not seeing what was right under her nose? Had she been so self-involved? Had she been that obsessed with Charlie that she had tuned out the entire world and what was going on around her?

Obviously she had, if she hadn't picked up that Ryan had feelings for her.

All she knew was that she had only one chance to make things up to him. If she blew it tonight, that was it. It was all over. She couldn't explain how she knew it, she just did. It was a feeling she had.

Her eyes darted through the crowded gym, and finally she saw him, standing by the refreshment table, sipping a glass of punch.

She blinked her eyes, as if seeing Ryan for the first time.

He was a wearing a dark, navy blue suit, with

an open-collared light blue shirt, looking very male model.

Why had she never before noticed how handsome he was? He glanced her way and when he saw her, he smiled. He put down his glass of punch and started walking toward her.

Why had she never noticed how great his smile was? How it lit up his entire face.

He looked happy.

And then it hit her.

She was the reason he was smiling.

She was why he was so happy.

And she'd never known.

Until today, she hadn't known!

As he got closer, she scrambled for something to say, but her mind was blank. *Think!* she silently screamed at herself. *Think!*

Seconds later he was standing in front of her and she was still speechless. Then her eyes fell on the wrist corsage she was wearing. Before she could stop herself, she held it up and waved it in Ryan's face. She wanted him to see that she was wearing his gift.

"It's pretty," he said.

"Thanks for sending it."

Ryan gave her a confused look, but before she could ask him about it, Simon, wearing a black suit, appeared before her, pointing at her wrist corsage.

"You wore it!" he happily exclaimed.

"Of course I did."

"Do you like it?" Simon asked.

"I love it," she said, looking at Ryan. "It was a very thoughtful gift."

Suddenly Ryan looked uncomfortable. Like he didn't know what to say. "Uh, Noelle?"

"Yes?"

"I didn't send the corsage."

He didn't send the corsage???

Before a shocked Noelle could say anything, Simon grabbed her by the hand, leading her out onto the dance floor as a new slow song began. "Come on, you promised me a dance."

"I did?" she asked, looking over her shoulder at Ryan. With her eyes, she pleaded for him to rescue her, but he remained where she'd left him.

"Yes, you did," Simon insisted, swaying to the music.

"But someone else would rather dance with you," Noelle said, her mind swirling. She didn't want to dance with Simon. She wanted to talk to Ryan! If Ryan hadn't sent her the corsage, then who did?

And why was Simon being so annoying? His hands were around her waist and he was pulling her close to him. *Much* too close. She pushed him away.

"Didn't you hear what I said?" she repeated. "Someone else would rather dance with you."

"Who?"

"Lily."

"Why would I want to dance with Lily?"

"Why wouldn't you? You told me today that you wanted to dance with her."

Simon shook his head. "No, I didn't."

"Yes, you did!"

Simon sighed. "Noelle, I would remember telling you that I wanted to dance with Lily."

"You said you wanted to dance with Connor's Secret Santa," she reminded him.

Simon nodded. "That's right. And I am!" he exclaimed, pulling Noelle back into his arms. "With you!"

"But I'm *not* Connor's Secret Santa," Noelle said, breaking free of Simon's embrace.

"You're not? Then who is?"

"Haven't you been listening to me? It's Lily!" Noelle shouted, hoping it would *finally* sink into Simon's thick head. "Lily!"

Lily heard Noelle shout her name as she walked into the dance. Looking around, she saw her on the dance floor with Simon. That was strange. The last person she expected to see Noelle dancing with was Simon.

She gave them a wave before heading in their direction. She couldn't wait to tell Noelle the juicy gossip she'd heard that afternoon at the hair salon when she'd gone for a shampoo and blow out. Her long curly hair was now sleek and straight, smoothly falling over one shoulder.

As she walked through the crowd, she could see some of the other girls checking out her outfit. Let them! She knew she looked good. She was wearing a black satin, strapless cocktail dress with a matching bolero jacket. And her shoes were adorable! Black satin, open-toed, with bows on the front.

As she drew closer to Simon and Noelle, she could hear Simon say, "Then if Lily is Connor's Secret Santa, that wrist corsage was meant for her and not you!" Simon then tore off the corsage of pink and white roses that was on Noelle's wrist and headed in her direction.

But before Simon could reach her, someone stepped in front of her, blocking her path.

It was Jason.

Her ex.

"Hey, Lily." He sounded nervous. And why shouldn't he? He'd broken her heart.

"Hey, Jason." Her voice wasn't friendly, but it wasn't cold either.

"You're looking good tonight."

"Thanks." Lily tried to walk around him, but every time she took a step, he matched it until finally she gave up. "Do you want something, Jason?" She tried not to sound impatient, but she was.

"I wanted to give you something."

"You wanted to give me something? What?" She laughed sarcastically. "More heartache?" She couldn't help herself. This was the closest she had been to him since before he went away for his summer job. When they were still a couple. Before he broke up with her without warning. If he expected her to be nice to him because it was Christmas, he was out of his mind!

"This," he said, placing half of a heart on a key chain into the palm of her hand.

Lily's eyes widened.

The heart was identical to the half heart she had received that morning.

"You?" she gasped. "You're my Secret Santa?"

Jason nodded. "Breaking up with you was the biggest mistake of my life. Can you ever forgive me, Lily? I miss you. I want to get back together. Will you please give me a second chance?"

Lily stared at the half of the heart in her hand. Then she handed it back to Jason. "I don't believe you. First you break up with me for Sonia, then you try to get back together with me while going out with her! What's the matter, Jason? Can't make up your mind? You broke my heart once. I'm not going to let you break it again. Besides, I already have a date for the dance."

She stepped around Jason and held out her wrist to Simon. "I think that corsage has my name on it?"

"It certainly does!"

As Simon slipped the corsage around her wrist, Lily turned back to Jason. "And how stupid do you think I am? I heard at the hair salon this afternoon that Sonia dumped you for her Secret Santa, Dennis Donahue!"

"What just happened?" Ryan asked, joining Noelle's side as Simon and Lily headed out onto the dance floor.

"Jason got his just deserts and Simon got his wires crossed," Noelle explained, turning to Ryan and gazing into his eyes. "Simon was crushing on the wrong person. Just the way I was . . ."

Chapter Twenty-Three

"What do you mean you were crushing on the wrong person?" Ryan asked.

How should she say this? Noelle didn't want Ryan to think he was her second choice, because he wasn't. He hadn't even been a choice! She just hadn't been interested in him or any other guys. Only Charlie.

All along Ryan had been telling her how awful Charlie was and she hadn't wanted to listen. Of course, Ryan wasn't so innocent. He'd constantly pointed out his big brother's faults because he had had his own agenda. He liked her!

And what girl didn't want to hear that a guy was interested in her?

Noelle decided that the best place to start was with the truth.

"I know," she told him.

"Know what?"

"That you're my Secret Santa."

"You do?" Ryan kept his face blank, not revealing anything. "Are you sure?"

"Positive." Noelle swatted Ryan on the arm. "Come on! Admit it!"

"What happens if I do?"

"You get to dance with me."

"Just a dance?"

Noelle pretended to think about it. "Well, you might get more than a dance. Maybe a kiss."

"Or two?"

"Maybe."

"What if you're wrong? What if it's not me?"

"But it is. I know it is."

"How do you know?"

Noelle pretended to lock her lips. "Can't tell you. It's a secret."

"You wouldn't mind if it was me?"

"Why would I mind!" Noelle exclaimed. "Those were the most wonderful gifts anyone has ever given me. I can't believe you went to so much trouble. Why would you do that?"

"I think you know why."

"I don't. Tell me," Noelle urged. She wanted to hear it. So much! "Please."

"I like you, Noelle. You're smart and you're pretty and you stand up to me! Even when we were little, you never took any of my crap!"

"Why didn't you ever tell me?"

Ryan shrugged. "I didn't realize it until just recently. But you know why I couldn't tell you."

Noelle sighed. "Charlie."

Ryan nodded. "You had a crush on him. A huge one. I had to hope that eventually you would get over it."

"Well, I have."

"What happened?"

"Everything you said finally sunk in."

Ryan gave Noelle a smile. "I'm glad to hear that."

Noelle smiled back. "Are you?"

Ryan closed the distance between himself and Noelle, taking her into his arms. "You know I am."

He was going to kiss her, Noelle realized. *He was going to kiss her!*

But before Ryan's lips could descend upon hers, they were distracted by the sound of yelling.

"What's going on?" Ryan asked, pulling away.

No! No! Noelle wanted to yell. *Come back! Come back and kiss me!*

"Let's see what's happening," Ryan said, taking Noelle by the hand and following everyone to a corner of the gym.

When they arrived, they saw Charlie with a blue-and-white scarf around his neck, sneezing like crazy. His eyes were red and watery and his nose was running. Standing by his side was his date, Liz Carmichael, who was poking a finger in Amber's chest.

"What's going on?" Noelle asked Lily, who was watching the scene with Simon.

"Amber revealed herself to Charlie as his Secret Santa and Liz is *not* happy about it," Simon told her. "She thinks Amber has been trying to steal her boyfriend."

"Why would she think that?" Ryan asked.

"Apparently Charlie's Secret Santa has been leaving Charlie *romantic* gifts and notes," Lily said, giving Noelle a look meant only for her. "Liz is out for blood!"

Noelle gulped. "She is?"

Lily nodded. "Hmmmhmmmm. Don't mess with a cheerleader!"

Noelle watched as Liz closed in on Amber, relieved that she wasn't on the receiving end of her wrath. Who knew Liz had such a temper!

"The game is over, honey," Liz said in a voice that meant business. "You've told Charlie you're his Secret Santa, now back off! He's *my* date for the dance."

Amber, who was wearing a silver-and-onyx sequin minidress, her long hair pulled into a sleek ponytail, poked a finger back into Liz's chest. "No one tells me what to do, got it? I'll go after any guy I want! What's the matter, Liz? Afraid of a little competition?"

Liz's eyes widened in outrage as she stared at the finger poking at her. "Oh, no, you didn't!" She slapped away Amber's finger and then gave her a shove. Amber crashed backward into a table filled with refreshments. "My boyfriend is off-limits! Especially to sneaky sophomores like you!"

Amber's arm fell into bowl of eggnog. "Look at what you did!" Amber screeched as she stared at her wet, dripping sleeve. Seconds later she was lunging at Liz with a banana crème pie, shoving it in her face. After that they were on the floor, kicking, clawing, and screaming at each other while everyone watched, choosing sides.

"This is way better than WWE wrestling!" Simon shouted.

"Look at what you did!" Lily hissed to Noelle. "This is all your fault!"

"My fault! How can you blame me? Liz is the one who shoved Amber!"

"Because she thought Amber was the one sending the gifts that *you* sent to Charlie!"

"Is it my fault that Liz is the jealous type?"

When the fight continued with no signs of letting up, Moose Novak ended it by dumping a bowl of punch over Amber and Liz. He also splashed Mindy Yee, who was standing on the sidelines with her digital camera and cell phone, alternating between taking pictures and sending text messages.

"You idiot!" Amber screamed as orange punch dripped down her dress. "Look at what you've done!"

"You've ruined my dress!" Liz shouted as she wiped punch off her face while Charlie continued sneezing.

"Mine, too!" Mindy wailed, abandoning her

camera and phone. "Do you know how much it cost?"

"Who cares about your ugly dresses?" Amber snapped.

"I can't believe what just happened!" Lily laughed as the crowd broke up and Principal Hicks arrived to deal with Amber and Liz while Moose began blotting Mindy's dress with a roll of paper towels. "Who knew there would be entertainment tonight?"

Celia raced over with Froggy. "What did we miss? What did we miss? We just got here!"

"A Christmas catfight!" Noelle announced.

Lily wiped tears of laughter away from her eyes. "I'm never going to forget this Christmas."

"Speaking of Christmas, do you guys want to hit the after-Christmas sales next week?" Celia asked. "Maybe catch a movie afterward?"

"I'd love it!" Noelle answered.

"Me too!" Lily agreed.

"A slow dance is starting," Froggy said, taking Celia by the hand.

"I'll talk to you guys later," Celia called out as she followed after Froggy.

"Feel like dancing?" Ryan asked Noelle.

"I'd love it!"

Shawna couldn't wait until the dance was over.

She was having a miserable time.

Everywhere she turned, she saw happy couples, as well as Secret Santas revealing themselves. She'd given Dennis Donahue his gift under the watchful glare of his new girlfriend, Sonia Lopez. Since he was such a jock, she'd bought him a subscription to *Sports Illustrated*, which he seemed to like.

Amber's real Secret Santa revealed himself to be Andrew O'Hallorhan, a very cute junior. But after seeing Amber doused with orange punch, Andrew didn't seem too interested in getting to know her. He gave her his gift — a box of chocolates — as Principal Hicks dragged her away, and then he asked Mindy Yee if she wanted to dance. That didn't make Moose Novak too happy because he turned out to be Mindy's Secret Santa and wanted to dance with her himself. Within minutes, Mindy was caught in a tug-of-war between Andrew and Moose which ended when the back of Mindy's wet dress ripped. Fortunately,

Mindy — who hadn't been able to make up her mind — had brought another dress to the dance and dashed to the girls' locker room to change into it.

Shawna sighed as she watched all the Christmas merriment around her. She had come to the dance alone and she was probably going to go home alone, even though she'd noticed some guys checking her out. She was wearing a strapless, burgundy lace dress and it looked *very* good on her, clinging in all the right places. But she wasn't interested in other guys! She was only interested in Connor! She'd been searching for him since she arrived, but didn't see him anywhere. She didn't know if that was good or bad. If he'd come to the dance solo, that was good. But if he'd come to the dance with a date, that was bad. The last thing she wanted to see was him with a date. That would mean things were officially over between them. They'd have broken up without having had a breakup.

Suddenly a pair of hands covered her eyes.

"Guess who?"

The voice was deep. Almost disguised. She didn't recognize it. Could it be Connor? She wanted it to be him but didn't dare hope.

"Did you know you're standing under the mistletoe?" the voice asked.

"I am?"

"Uh-huh. You know what that means."

"You get a kiss," Shawna said.

"Yep. Ready to pay up?"

"I'm ready."

Shawna turned around and found herself facing David. He'd cleaned up very nicely in the new outfit they'd bought the day before. But he was still David. He wasn't Connor.

"Gee, you don't have to look so disappointed," he said. "It's only a kiss. It's not like you have to marry me."

"I'm not upset about having to kiss you. Honest. I was hoping you were someone else, that's all." She pointed upward. "Standing under the mistletoe entitles you to one kiss. So kiss away."

That was all David needed to hear as he swooped in and planted his lips on Shawna's.

Shawna braced herself for a full facial assault. But the kiss wasn't as bad as she thought it would be. Actually, it was pretty nice. She'd expected it to be all wet and messy. Slobbery. The way a Saint Bernard would lick your face. Instead,

David's kiss was soft. Gentle. But with just enough pressure to let you know that he knew what he was doing.

Who would have thought he was such an excellent kisser?

David could tell she hadn't minded the kiss. After all, she hadn't wiped the back of her hand against her mouth.

"See what you've been missing," he said. "There's more where that came from. If you're interested."

"If anyone is going to be kissing Shawna, it's me."

Shawna whirled around and found herself facing Connor.

Who was alone!

Did that mean . . .

She didn't dare hope!

"So," he asked, handing her a wrapped gift, "are you wearing the peppermint lip gloss the way I asked?"

Shawna's mouth dropped open. "You're my Secret Santa?!"

Connor gave her a wide smile, showing off those two dimples that she loved. "I am!"

That meant he still cared about her.

He wouldn't have left her such sweet gifts if he didn't.

And he wouldn't have said he wanted to kiss her if he wanted to break up with her!

Shawna threw her arms around Connor and began kissing him all over his face. "You are *such* a sweetie!"

"I'm sorry I haven't been around the last couple of weeks," he said. "But I had a reason."

"You did?"

"I was working so much because I wanted to buy you a really special Christmas present."

The present! Shawna had forgotten all about it!

She unwrapped the box Connor had given to her and when she opened it she found a beautiful silver ring with a floral design.

"I love it!" she exclaimed.

Connor took the ring out of the box and slipped it onto her finger.

It fit perfectly!

"I hope this means we're going steady," he said. "Unless you're going out with someone else?" Connor tilted his dark head in David's direction.

"David's just a friend," she said. And she

meant it. She'd enjoyed spending time with him the last couple of days and getting to know him.

"So we're going steady?"

"Absolutely!" she happily gushed, holding out her hand and admiring the ring. "I love it so much! And I love you!"

"So how about a Christmas dance?" Connor asked.

"Bye, David," Shawna called over her shoulder as she followed after Connor. "I'll give you that dance I owe you later. Promise."

David stood on the edge of the dance floor with a sad smile on his face. He really thought he might have had a chance with Shawna, but once again jock trumped nerd. Even Froggy had a date! And with Celia! How had that happened?!

Then he felt a tap on his shoulder.

He turned around and saw it was Shawna's younger sister, Chloe. She'd glammed herself up from the last time he'd seen her, wearing a violet-colored baby-doll dress. Gone were her glasses, and her hair was soft and flowing. He almost didn't recognize her.

In fact, she looked pretty.

Very pretty.

She gave him a smile.

A real smile.

Like she was happy to see him.

David looked over his shoulder, just to make sure she wasn't smiling at someone else.

"How about dancing with your Secret Santa?" she asked.

David's mouth dropped open.

Chloe moved closer to David and pointed upward. "And how about a kiss? Did you know you're standing under the mistletoe?"

Before David could answer, Chloe threw her arms around him in a hug and gave him a big fat kiss.

"So can I ask you a question?" Celia asked Freddy.

"Shoot."

"How'd you get your nickname?"

Froggy blushed. "When I was in kindergarten I wore a frog costume for Halloween and I didn't want to take it off for weeks. Whenever my mom tried to take it off, I threw a tantrum. Finally she just gave up and let me wear it everywhere.

Because of that, the kids started calling me Froggy and the name stuck."

"Is it okay if I keep calling you Freddy?" Celia asked. "Or do you like Froggy better?"

"You can call me anything you want," Froggy said.

"Merry Christmas, Freddy," Celia said, giving him a kiss.

"So are you and Amber officially broken up?" Lily asked Simon as they danced.

Simon thought about the question. "Well, let's see. Amber was using the Secret Santa game to find a new boyfriend to replace me. In case you hadn't heard, she wanted a hot senior."

"You're pretty hot yourself," Lily said.

"It's nice to know someone thinks so. Unofficially, Amber and I broke up weeks ago, but we never told each other. I was waiting until the new year and she was waiting until tonight. I think it's safe to say we're now officially broken up. Why? Know anyone who's interested in a boyfriend?"

"Why don't we start with a date first?" Lily suggested. "Make sure you know what you're getting. It wasn't that long ago that you were interested in my best friend."

"I was interested in you first," Simon said. "Then I got confused and thought Noelle was Connor's Secret Santa and so I transferred my feelings for you over to Noelle."

"A likely story."

"It's true." Simon pressed his forehead against Lily's, gazing into her eyes. "I know Jason hurt you, Lily, but I'm not the kind of guy who cheats."

"What kind of guy are you?"

Simon leaned closer to Lily and whispered into her ear. "I'm the kind of guy who wants to have one special girl in his life. Think I might get that this Christmas?"

"Maybe you will," Lily whispered into his ear, deciding that it was time to take another chance on love. "Maybe you will."

"So you're my Secret Santa, huh?" Noelle said to Ryan as they were dancing. "Well guess what?"

"What?"

"You're dancing with *your* Secret Santa."

"So where's my present?"

"How about dinner and a movie?"

"You mean like a date?"

Noelle thought about it and then nodded. "Like a date."

Ryan pulled her closer. "How did you figure it out?" he asked.

"Never mind how I figured it out. Are you willing to give me another chance or have you given up on me?" Noelle held up the gold key Ryan had sent her that morning. "Does this still work?"

"It still works, Noelle. But only if you want it to."

"I do."

"If I'd given up on you, I wouldn't have sent you all those gifts. Besides, it's Christmas. The time of year when anything is possible."

"Even a Christmas kiss?" Noelle shyly asked as she gazed into Ryan's eyes and saw the way he was looking at her. He was *into* her. *So* into her. And she had been too blind to notice.

But not anymore.

"Even a Christmas kiss," Ryan said as his lips met Noelle's and he gave her exactly what she wanted for Christmas.

Here's a sneak peek at another cozy winter read:

Kissing Snowflakes

by Abby Sher

Beep beep!

"Hey, kid, you want a lift?" Dad pulled up to the curb in a bright blue rental Explorer, and stuck his head out the window like an eager puppy. My brother, Jeremy, was in the back, staring out the opposite window. Kathy was in the passenger seat, a wide smile plastered across her face.

"Sure," I said, throwing my duffel in the trunk. I was the last one out from the baggage carousel because they had thought my bag was missing. That's kind of how I felt today, like a lost, limp bag, on my way to who knows where. I climbed in next to Jeremy.

"The fun starts now, kids!" said Dad. His eyes went back and forth between the two of us in the rearview mirror. They were so wide and hopeful, and I could see how important it was for him that this be true.

"Yippee!" said Kathy, clapping her hands.

Dad wound his way out of the Burlington, Vermont, airport and onto the open road. The mountains rose up around us, great snowy peaks etched against a lilac sky. It was already afternoon. The sun hung low, slowly sifting into fiery reds and oranges, spreading its warm glow over everything. It really was beautiful. Dad navigated us through the roads swiftly and smoothly. He was an excellent driver. So steady and calm. I always felt safe with him at the wheel.

"Ah, isn't that breathtaking?" he sighed, reaching for Kathy's hand out over the console.

"This is gonna be a total blast!" she said, leaning on his arm.

I wanted to tell her that nobody said "total blast" anymore. I think that went out soon after "gag me with a spoon." But I kept my mouth shut and just sighed to myself.

I knew I was being a snot. I knew I should've been enjoying the view, feeling the rush of the clear Vermont air, losing myself in the majestic trees towering above us, draped in their dresses of snow. But I felt miserable, watching Dad and Kathy all snuggly in the front seat. Her shiny dark hair fell over her shoulders and she was oohing and aahing as Dad steered us through patches of trees, winding past sleepy villages with tall church steeples, lopsided wooden fences, and an old-fashioned pharmacy called Canfield Corners.

Dad and Kathy. Kathy and Dad.

How had we come here?

Well, we had just flown in from Florida, where Dad and Kathy got married.

Wait. Back up.

It started that night when Mom and Dad announced they were taking some time to "find themselves." Dad was pacing around the dinner table with his hands in his back pockets. He wouldn't sit still. Mom was pushing her lamb chop back and forth across the plate. Jeremy was chewing his Tater Tots — with his mouth open, of course. He always chewed with his mouth open even though he was two years older than me. Mom usually asked him to please close his mouth while he was eating. Dad did, too. But that night, nobody said anything about it.

"So, Mom and I have been talking and let me start this by saying that this came after some long and hard thought. We have really tried to make this work and we don't know what to do right now except this. And I mean, it doesn't feel right, but really nothing has felt right for a long time. For a long, long time. And so . . . well, we've decided to separate for a while. So, this is just for now. Or for — jeesh, I'm doing a lot of talking. Sarah, do you want to add anything?"

Mom shook her head. Her gray hair swished and then fell back into place and she tucked it behind her ears, but she wouldn't look up from her plate.

"Do you have any questions for us? Jeremy? Samantha?" That's me. Samantha. Samantha Iris Levy. Usually everybody calls me Sam, though. And when I'm talking to myself, I call myself Levy. I know, it's kinda weird. But there you have it.

That was so long ago now. Four years ago, to be exact. Even though it felt like it was yesterday. Even though I could taste it in the back of my throat and feel it pulling my stomach into a tight knot. My hands were sweating and I felt like an overgrown marshmallow in my ski jacket.

It had all happened so fast after that.

Mom stayed in our house (in a little suburb in Westchester, New York), Dad moved about ten minutes away into Chatsworth Towers. His apartment was so small that he made us eggs for dinner and we had to eat them standing up. About a year later, Grandpa got sick, and Dad said he needed to go down to Florida to take care of him. It was supposed to be just for a little while. But the next thing we knew he was moving into his own place down in Orlando, and it had a screened-in porch and a bird feeder where he could see blue jays every morning. Jeremy and I went to visit for a weekend and the whole time Dad had his binoculars out, showing us the difference between the crested flycatcher and the purple martin.

Then he started working at Simmons & Cray as one of the chief financial officers. He said the work was very challenging, an easy commute, and did he mention that he rescued a tree swallow that had fallen out of a branch and that he had started seeing a wonderful woman named Kathy? She was a travel agent, and we would definitely like her because she was a Yankees fan and really into the outdoors and she had a cat named Annette. I tried to tell him that he didn't like cats, but Dad just said, "I thought I didn't. But this is different. Things are different now."

I asked him when he was moving back, and he said the weather was always sunny, even in October, and then November, and then December.

December 27.

Dad and Kathy set the wedding date so that Jeremy and I could come down for winter break. We flew out on Christmas because Dad found a cheap flight, and besides it's not like we were missing anything, because we're Jewish. Kathy came with Dad to pick us up from the airport in her little red hatchback. Everything about Kathy was petite and perky. She had warm, caramel-colored skin and dark, sparkling eyes above her perfect, tiny nose. When we got out of the car at the condo, she came up to my shoulder.

The wedding was in a little Mexican restaurant in Orlando, because Kathy's family is Mexican. They were married by a justice of the peace, and Dad had this big drooly grin on his face the whole time and then we had really bad Mexican food.

So, that was the story, more or less. And here we were. This was going to be winter break. The four of us were headed to an inn in West Lake, Vermont, for a week of skiing and sitting by the fire, and "getting to know each other." Ugh. I didn't even know how to ski. I had a feeling it wasn't going to come naturally either. I liked running in gym, and I had gone to ballet classes when I was little, but most of the time I was trying not to trip over my own feet. To me, downhill skiing sounded like an invitation to a face dive. Jeremy was psyched, though. He had been skiing a few times with friends and said this time he was going to try snow-boarding, too. Dad and Kathy were going to do cross-country, because they heard that was easier to break into. So that left me all alone.

I did have a plan, though. Phoebe and I had talked about it for weeks before. Phoebe was my best friend and we told each other *everything*. She said West Lake was the capital for hot snow studs, and she was sure I was going to find one at the inn. Then I wouldn't have to worry about Kathy or Dad or anybody. I had visions of myself flying down the mountain, my scarf whipping behind me, a tall, dark-haired Adonis holding me firmly by the waist. Or he could be blond. And he didn't have to have muscles. Big muscles kind of ook me out anyway. Just tall. He had to be taller than me. Which meant six feet at least.

Everybody in my family is tall. Dad is 6'2".

Jeremy is 6'1". Mom is 5'9" and so am I. It really sucks because most of the guys in my grade are barely my height. Everything about me is kind of long and stringy. My arms, my legs, my hair — which is the color of mud and somewhere between flat and flatter. And I got these long, droopy ears from my dad. That's why I keep my hair long, and I never wear ponytails. It's too embarrassing. Jeremy has the same ears, but he's a boy so he doesn't care. We also both have a bunch of freckles on our faces. The one thing I actually like about myself is my gray eyes. I'm the only one in my family who has them. My mom says they're exotic. But I think she says that mostly because she's my mom. Anyway, I have a thing for eyes. It's the first thing I notice about people. And I dream about the day when some-one will stare all gaga into mine.

It had been so long since I had been with some-one. It had been since like — okay, ever. Unless you counted the school play, *The Grapes of Wrath*, where I got to kiss Leo Strumm. He was playing Al, and I was Al's Girl and there was this scene where I said, "I thought you said I was purty," and then he had to kiss me. It was my first real kiss. I mean, I know I'm almost sixteen years old and most people have kissed by then, but I guess I'm a late bloomer and nobody knew it except for Phoebe and my mom but . . . yeah, there it is.

I had practiced long and hard for that kiss. I made Phoebe sit up with me on my bed and we had smothered my pillows with slobbery smooches. It was a good thing that Phoebe was patient. She's definitely more experienced than me. She's just more comfortable around guys than I am. She has red curly hair and cobalt-blue eyes and really pale skin that gets splotches of color whenever she laughs too hard. And she's good at making conversation, cracking jokes, even walking up to complete strangers at parties and introducing herself.

But not me. I don't know what it is. I usually have something to say about *everything*. Seriously. Mom says it's good that I have opinions. And I do make Phoebe and my other friend Rachel laugh. I know how to say *Please take me to your home. I will be a good wife,* in Russian. But around guys I feel like my mouth is full of fuzzy marbles. Sometimes Phoebe has to pinch me in the arm just so I'll say hello. Lately, I've been thinking I should just wear a sign that says *Really, I'm interesting. Give me a chance. P.S. If I pass out, I'm type O-positive.*

Phoebe has kissed a bunch of guys, even dated

a few. But a lot of kids in our grade are way ahead of both of us. Like having sex and stuff. Sara Spencer and Kevin Mallon have done it. So have Alissa Paulson and Andy Trotts. And almost everyone on the girls' lacrosse team lost their virginity on the tournament weekend down in Alexandria, Virginia. Meanwhile, I still have Cookie Monster slippers and I like to sleep with my favorite little pillow — but I hope I'll catch up one day soon. At this rate, I'll probably start having sex when I turn forty.

Phoebe said not to give up. That I had to change my attitude. Maybe I was trying too hard. Or not hard enough. I just had to act like myself and act like I *liked* myself and then guys would see that I was fun to be around. And so we had made a pact. This winter break, something was going to happen. We were going to *make* it happen. We were going to wear our shiniest lip gloss and put on our brightest smiles. And we were going to find ourselves some men. Some *real* men.

"Ooh, look at that!" cried Kathy. Two deer leaped across a field after each other, circling playfully around a clump of trees. Hmmrgh. Even deer could find love out here in the woods. There *had* to be someone for me, too, right?

"Did you see that?" Kathy asked, turning around in her seat. Jeremy was asleep, so she looked at me, her eyelashes batting wildly.

"Yeah, we have deer where I grew up, too," I said. I knew it was mean, but I was not in the mood.

Kathy seemed unfazed. "It's just so magical," she sighed, turning around again. "You know what my favorite thing to do is when it's snowing really hard?" she continued.

"What?" asked Dad.

"I love to go outside and spend the afternoon kissing snowflakes."

Dad gave a soft chuckle. "Kissing snowflakes?"

"Yeah! You know, you tilt your head up to the sky and you just let them fall on you. And a lot of them land on your nose or maybe in your eyes and melt. But when you get one, when you really catch the right one on your lips, you *know*."

I could see in the mirror Dad had one of those dumb smiles on his face like at the wedding. Ugh.

"I guess it's kinda silly when I say it out loud," Kathy said, softer now.

"Yup," I mouthed, even though nobody was looking at me.

To Do List: Read All the Point Books!

By Aimee Friedman

☐ South Beach
0-439-70678-5

☐ French Kiss
0-439-79281-9

☐ Hollywood Hills
0-439-79282-7

By Abby Sher

☐ Kissing Snowflakes
0-545-00010-6

By Hailey Abbott

☐ Summer Boys
0-439-54020-8

☐ Next Summer: A
Summer Boys Novel
0-439-75540-9

☐ After Summer: A
Summer Boys Novel
0-439-86367-8

☐ Last Summer: A
Summer Boys Novel
0-439-86725-8

By Claudia Gabel

☐ In or Out
0-439-91853-7

☐ Loves Me, Loves Me Not:
An In or Out Novel
0-439-91854-5

By Nina Malkin

☐ 6X: The
Uncensored
Confessions
0-439-72421-X

☐ 6X: Loud, Fast,
& Out of Control
0-439-72422-8

☐ Orange Is the New
Pink
0-439-89965-6

By Pamela Wells

☐ The Heartbreakers
0-439-02691-1

Point

SCHOLASTIC and associated logos are trademarks and/or registered trademarks of Scholastic Inc.

I ♥ Bikinis Series

- ☐ I ♥ Bikinis:
  He's with Me
  By Tamara Summers
  0-439-91850-2

- ☐ I ♥ Bikinis:
  Island Summer
  By Jeanine Le Ny
  0-439-91851-0

- ☐ I ♥ Bikinis:
  What's Hot
  By Caitlyn Davis
  0-439-91852-9

By Erin Haft

- ☐ Pool Boys
  0-439-83523-2

By Laura Dower

- ☐ Rewind
  0-439-70340-9

By Jade Parker

- ☐ To Catch a Pirate
  0-439-02694-6

By Randi Reisfeld and H.B. Gilmour

- ☐ Oh Baby!
  0-439-67705-X

By Sabrina James

- ☐ Secret Santa
  0-439-02695-4

Story Collections

- ☐ Fireworks: Four
  Summer Stories
  By Niki Burnham, Erin Haft,
  Sarah Mlynowski, and
  Lauren Myracle
  0-439-90300-9

- ☐ 21 Proms
  Edited by Daniel Ehrenhaft
  and David Levithan
  0-439-89029-2

- ☐ Mistletoe: Four Holiday
  Stories
  By Hailey Abbott,
  Melissa de la Cruz, Aimee
  Friedman, and Nina Malkin
  0-439-86368-6

www.thisispoint.com